'My, my,' Michael lea... looking down at her, a......... plainly flickering in his eyes. 'You do get all het up, don't you, Miss Kempson!'

'Yes, I do,' said Gabbie coldly, 'especially when there are some doctors about like you, who think they're God, and that nurses are merely menial subjects, put on this earth for the sole purpose of fetching and carrying at their command!'

'Aren't they?' he said. 'I thought they were.'

'Well, that's where you're wrong!' hissed Gabbie, now almost beside herself with rage. 'One day the twentieth century will even reach Crete and the women here, then look out!'

'I shouldn't count on it,' said Michael with a mischievous smile. 'I believe there is a distinct place on earth for men and women, and it's clearly defined that man shall be the master.'

'Oh . . . !' Gabbie picked up the nearest book and threw it, missing him as he closed the door smartly behind him; the book fell with a dull thud to the floor. Gabbie stared at the book, then the thought occurred to her, perhaps he really did want to drive her away. Well, if that's your little game, she thought defiantly, it won't work. She had promised Paulos she would stay, and stay she would, no matter how objectionable his son might be!

Ann Jennings has been married for twenty-nine years and worked in a hospital for thirteen years —accounting for the technicalities accurately described in her hospital romances. Her son is a medical student and often provides her with amusing titbits of information. Hospitals are romantic places she maintains, romance blossoms where two people share a common interest. REALLY, DOCTOR! is her seventh Doctor Nurse Romance. Recent titles include RUN-AWAY SISTER, DOCTOR'S ORDERS and NURSE ON LOAN.

REALLY, DOCTOR!

BY

ANN JENNINGS

MILLS & BOON LIMITED
ETON HOUSE 18–24 PARADISE ROAD
RICHMOND SURREY TW9 1 SR

First published in Great Britain 1987 by Mills & Boon Limited

© Ann Jennings 1987

Australian copyright 1987 Philippine copyright 1987

ISBN 0 263 75969 5

Set in 11 on 12 pt Linotron Times
03–0188–45,800

Photoset by Rowland Phototypesetting Limited Bury St Edmunds, Suffolk Made and printed in Great Britain by William Collins Sons & Co Limited, Glasgow

CHAPTER ONE

'REALLY, Dr Nikolaides!'

'You seem surprised, Miss Kempson.'

Olive black eyes gleamed, locked in hostile conflict with Gabrielle Kempson's sapphire blue ones. Normally they were as blue and sparkling as a sunlit lagoon, but now they glittered with blue fire, hard as the stones their colour resembled, as she regarded the tall dark man leaning on the desk in front of her.

'You heard the question?' Michael Nikolaides' voice was laced with sardonic amusement as he leaned back in his chair and regarded the tall, fair-haired girl who sat before him. But his fingers drumming an impatient tattoo on the desk top gave lie to the calm smoothness of his voice. He was annoyed, and she knew why—he had met his match! She smiled grimly, a tall blonde girl, not intimidated by him in the least; quite the contrary, in fact, she almost relished a fight, and had sensed hostility from the moment the interview had begun.

Gabrielle Kempson, Gabbie to her friends, sat seething with fury, regarding the enormous dark man sitting opposite her with something closely akin to intense loathing. He was huge, completely dominating the small room, his skin swarthy, his nose prominent, in fact beaky, thought Gabbie

acidly. It was given more prominence by the fact
that there were hollows beneath the high cheek-
bones, which in turn made the aggressive jut of
his jaw more pronounced. His mouth was wide
and sensual, and at that moment shut tight in a
hard uncompromising line as he waited for her
answer.

Not for the first time that morning, she wished
she had never agreed to her brother Peter's bright
idea of being interviewed for the job of senior
Sister, running a small private paediatric hospital in
Crete; but then on reflection and being realistic she
knew why. It was a question of beggars not being
able to be choosers; she had been made redundant
by the closure of the large London paediatric hospital in which she had worked ever since qualifying
and then training in paediatrics. She had known no
other life than that of nursing children, and wanted
no other; having long ago decided that she was a
career girl, and a marriage and a home was not for
her. Her brother always teased her, saying it was
her Freudian desire for children of her own that
made her want to look after other people's, something she always hotly denied. But she couldn't
deny the fact that being with children gave her
more pleasure than anything else, and that was
why, when she had been offered a post at the same
salary in a different London teaching hospital, but a
general nursing post, not paediatric, she had turned
it down, thus placing herself in the ranks of the
unemployed.

When Peter had told her about Dr Paulos

Nikolaides, a friend of his, who ran a clinic on Crete, it had seemed like the answer to her prayers. A job with children, and a new place to work, somewhere other than London where she had been ever since she had started her training at eighteen. Now, at twenty-six, she realised that she hadn't done very much with her life, except rush from her rather spartan flat backwards and forwards to hospitals. Crete had seemed an attractive alternative.

She thought about it in the past tense—*had* being the operative word. What her brother had failed to mention was that charming Dr Paulos Nikolaides, whom she had fallen in love with on sight, had a huge, objectionable son, who obviously thought nurses were one of the lowest forms of life! Great Greek gorilla! she thought venomously, flashing him another shower of blue sparks from her blazing eyes.

'I'm still waiting.' The tattoo beaten by the long, darkly tanned fingers increased in tempo.

'Michael!' The older man sitting beside his son turned and raised a hand in mild rebuke. He smiled at Gabbie, trying to put her at her ease again; his eyes were dark too, but warm and limpid, not arrogant and quelling like those of his son. 'Michael worries about the clinic. He worries about me getting the right Sister for the job.' He chuckled in a self-deprecating manner. 'To tell you the truth, Gabbie—I hope I may call you that,' he added, 'he doesn't say so, but in reality he thinks I'm getting a little too long in the tooth for the job of running the place!'

A reluctant smile flickered across Gabbie's face; for a moment her blue eyes softened and her generous mouth curved with a gentle warmth. She would get on well with elderly Dr Paulos, she had intuitively known that the moment she had met him. Much the same as she had just as surely known that she and Michael Nikolaides would mix about as well as fire and water!

When she had first met seventy-year-old Dr Paulos over an informal drink with her brother, she had wanted the job. Now she was not so sure, nothing had been mentioned about the objectionable Michael by Dr Paulos, so it had come as a very unpleasant surprise when he had been present at the interview, and indeed had taken most of the initiative in the questioning. That was the problem, it was not only the questions, but the manner in which he asked them.

'I'm sorry if my question stunned you,' Michael Nikolaides' voice cut across her straying thoughts. He smiled, a great flash of white teeth in the dark expanse of his face, and his voice had a more conciliatory tone to it.

Don't try and charm me, you great bully, thought Gabbie coldly, rewarding his smile with an icy glance that would have frozen most men on the spot. It bounced off the great bulk of Michael Nikolaides, however, with an almost audible 'plink' as he continued to smile and strum the table top.

'Yes, I suppose you could say I was stunned.' Her full mouth tightened as she spoke, and her tone was clipped and precise. 'Stunned at the idiotic nature of the question!'

'How could a paediatric nurse, trained in hi-tech methods, cope with an emergency without any sophisticated equipment?' He paused, the smile disappeared abruptly, the olive eyes glittered menacingly, and the rhythmic drumming of his fingers suddenly stopped, leaving a sudden pregnant stillness in the room. 'I do not consider that an idiotic question.'

Tilting her oval chin defiantly, Gabbie brushed a stray wisp of her long fine hair back from her face, her eyes meeting the challenge of his head-on.

'The whole point is that I am a *trained* paediatric nurse,' she snapped. 'In England where I've done all my training, we're taught to cope with any eventuality. Hi-tech equipment, as you call it, is there as an aid, not a substitute for nursing.' She raised her finely arched dark brows. 'You may not believe me, Dr Nikolaides, but even here in England, there's not always hi-tech equipment available to assist during an emergency. I have no qualms about my ability to handle any situation without losing my head. Of course,' she added on a scathing note, 'whether or not I'd match up to your exacting standards is quite another matter! In fact,' she stood up abruptly, flicking at an imaginary speck on her skirt with her gloves—the wretched man was beginning to get her rattled, 'I'm beginning to think this whole interview is a waste of time. I'm obviously not the sort of person you're looking for.'

'Oh no, no!' Dr Paulos stood up, and hurried around the desk. He put a fatherly arm around Gabbie's shoulders. 'You are just what I am looking for.' He glowered at his son, and for a fraction of a second Gabbie saw the same steely glint as she had seen in Michael Nikolaides' eyes, the same determination. 'I am going to offer Miss Kempson the post, Michael.'

His son shrugged his massive shoulders dismissively. 'As you please. You will be working with her, not me.' He wandered over to the window as if dismissing the subject completely, and stood looking out, his back to them.

'Thank you for the vote of confidence,' Gabbie couldn't resist saying, 'and what do you mean, you won't be working with me?'

'Come along, my dear, this has been a long morning,' Dr Paulos said hastily, trying to pour oil on troubled waters. 'Let's go and have lunch, and I'll show you some photographs and tell you all about the Institute.' He started to shepherd Gabbie from the room.

'Do you mean there aren't any other appplicants?' Gabbie stood still, rooted to the spot with astonishment.

'No, you got it the easy way. A piece of cake, is the English expression, I believe!' Michael's voice rang with ill-concealed rancour. 'Dad made up his mind about you when he met you and your brother. That's why I came along to the interview, just to make sure he wasn't making an awful mistake.'

'And do you think he has?' asked Gabbie

quietly. Suddenly, for some reason she couldn't explain, it had become desperately important to have the son's approval too, and not just that of Dr Paulos.

'Only time will tell,' was the answer she had to be content with, as he turned and looked at her through narrowed eyes, summing her up.

Involuntarily Gabbie drew herself up to her full height of five feet six inches, tallish as most girls went, but even so she barely reached the height of Michael Nikolaides' shoulders. 'I shall do my best,' she assured him stiffly.

'I'm sure you will.' His mouth curled in an amused smile at the military precision of her stance. 'You look like the typically efficient Nordic type,' he added, and before Gabbie had time to digest the remark and work out whether it was meant as a compliment or not, he had turned from her to his father. 'Excuse me if I don't join you for lunch, but I have another appointment, at the American Embassy.'

His father nodded. 'Of course, I'd forgotten. But don't worry, Gabbie and I will get along famously.'

Michael raised one eyebrow in an ironic quirk of agreement as he turned back to Gabbie. 'Goodbye, Miss Kempson,' he said.

'Goodbye, Dr Nikolaides.' The temptation to add 'good riddance' was almost overwhelming, but Gabbie kept her wayward tongue in check and managed a stiff smile as he left the room—covering the distance, she noticed, with just three long, athletic strides.

Later, over lunch, Dr Paulos, as he insisted Gabbie should call him, explained that the Kriti Institute, near Aghios Nikolaos, was a small fifty-bedded paediatric hospital, privately owned and run by him and another doctor, an American called Sam Jones.

'You only treat private patients?' asked Gabbie, a forkful of food poised halfway to her mouth. She hadn't realised it was private, and was not sure she wanted to work only for the rich.

'We treat whoever needs to be treated,' replied Dr Paulos firmly. 'Patients who are insured or wealthy pay for their treatment, as it is in the rest of Greece, but those who are poor get treatment free—paid for by a trust fund that was set up when the Institute was first built. I pride myself that no one in need has ever been turned away. So you needn't worry, my dear, you won't only be treating the pampered children of the rich!' He had read her thoughts very accurately.

Gabbie smiled; was she so transparent? 'And Michael?' she enquired, trying to sound casual, 'where does he fit into the picture?'

'In two years' time he will take over directorship of the Institute when I retire, but until then he has a Research Fellowship in Denver, Colorado, at the Children's Hospital there. That is why he couldn't join us for lunch, he has visas and papers to get sorted out at the Embassy—you know the sort of thing.'

'Yes,' said Gabbie wryly, 'I know the sort of thing.'

Perhaps he did have a visa to sort out, but she'd have put money on the fact that even if he hadn't, he would have found some other plausible excuse for missing lunch. He didn't like her, he didn't approve of her, she'd known that the minute she'd clapped eyes on him, and it had been mutual. Oh well, she reflected, at least she knew her job in Crete would last two years. The minute Michael came back to take over, she would leave; in a small fifty-bedded hospital there wouldn't be room for both of them!

'All the nurses speak English of sorts,' said Dr Paulos, his voice breaking into her thoughts, 'and I was wondering whether it would be possible for you to make arrangements to fly out at the end of the week—next week, I mean. It's not much notice, I know, but I do need you.'

Gabbie nodded. There was no reason why not; she was unemployed, after all. 'I have to give one week's notice for my flat,' she said, 'and it won't take me long to get organised. I'll pop down to say goodbye to my mother in Truro. Peter's here, so I'll be seeing him. No, it won't take me long at all.'

She sighed, No, it wouldn't take long. She doubted whether her mother would have time to see her anyway, she was always so tied up with her work as consultant psychiatrist in Truro—always seeming to have unlimited time for her patients, but no time at all for Gabbie or Peter; and he could do with some help and advice at the moment, Gabbie reflected miserably.

'I'm sorry about Peter and Sue, my dear.' Dr

Paulos hadn't missed the quiet little sigh. 'I've known your brother a long time, ever since he did his elective in Athens, and if there is anything I can do to help, to reconcile him and his wife, I will do it.'

Gabbie looked at him gratefully, trying to choke back the tears that suddenly threatened. Peter, Sue and their little daughter Emma had been the one stable element in her life, her brother's seemingly happy marriage had made up for the home she had never had, and she had spent many happy hours at the rambling Victorian house in Dulwich. But she had seen the danger signs, and had tried to warn Peter that he was spending too much time at the hospital, where he was one of two consultant urologists, and not enough time with Sue and Emma. But his reply had always been that Sue understood, and when his elderly colleague, who was near to retirment, had put more and more of the work-load on Peter's shoulders, it seemed he never got home. In the end it proved too much for Sue; she had left and gone back to her mother, taking little Emma with her.

'There's just no point in being married,' Sue had said sadly as Gabbie had tried to persuade her to stay. 'Peter's too tired to notice when he comes home whether we're here or not. We're not really married, we just happen to live in the same house.'

'I would never have thought that Peter would end up like Mother, devoted to the hospital at the expense of his family life,' observed Gabbie quietly.

She knew that Peter had talked to Dr Paulos a lot when he had been younger, because he had told her so, regarding the older man as the father he had never had. Dr Paulos knew their unhappy background—mother too interested in psychiatry to have time for her children, father too interested in writing travel novels to take time off to come back home. Her parents had stayed married, although Gabbie had often wondered why, as neither seemed to care now whether they ever saw each other again; and both she and Peter had been shunted from one boarding school to another. Once she had started her training, she had taken up permanent residence in London, only occasionally going to Truro to see her mother. She smiled bitterly, remembering the last occasion, her mother's birthday. She had written to tell her she was coming, planning to take her out for a special dinner; but her mother had forgotten and had gone off to a conference in Edinburgh, and Gabbie had had no alternative but to turn around and come back to London.

'There's still time for things to be sorted out,' Dr Paulos' voice broke into her unhappy thoughts. 'Wait and see.' He smiled and put his hand on hers. 'And what about you, my dear, how long shall I be able to keep you in Crete? Or are you planning to be married in the near future?'

Gabbie shook her head. 'Never,' she said vehemently. 'I decided long ago that I was cut out to be a career girl. I'm definitely not cut out for domesticity.'

'Hmm . . .' murmured Dr Paulos with a gentle smile, taking a sip of his wine, his dark eyes regarding her with some amusement over the rim of his glass.

'I mean it,' she said, a defiant note edging into her voice. 'I shall never get married.'

She did mean it, she never wanted to get close enough to anyone to get hurt. Because in spite of everything, she knew the real reason her mother had buried herself in her work. It was because she had been bitterly hurt by her father. Once, when she had been very little, she had found her mother weeping over one of her father's novels, and had had the temerity to ask her if Daddy still loved them.

'He never loved us,' her mother had replied harshly, 'and especially he never loved me.'

After that, her mother had never spoken of their father again, seemingly regretting her outburst. She had condemned herself and her children to a barren emotional life, and Peter and Gabbie only had each other, and as a result had become very close. That was why Gabbie felt so badly about Peter's marriage breaking up. She couldn't bear to see him unhappy, and the worst thing was that it was partly his own fault. Perhaps if she got away to Crete, she would be able to see things more objectively, and then be able to help her brother; the thought gave her some comfort.

'I'm glad you have no immediate plans.' She jumped, suddenly aware that she had been nervously pleating the edge of the tablecloth, so immersed had she been with her own thoughts. Dr Paulos smiled again. That means that you'll stay with us in Crete for some time, I hope. Although as far as marriage is concerned, never is a long time!'

'I'm looking forward to it,' said Gabbie truthfully, ignoring his comment about never being a long time. She looked out of the window of the restaurant where cold spring rain lashed against the glass, running down the pane like tears. 'Will it be warm yet?'

Dr Paulos threw back his head and roared with laughter. 'I think you are in for a big surprise,' he told her. 'Will it be warm indeed!'

'Will what be warm?' A deep, rich voice from behind Gabbie interrupted the laughter.

Swinging round in her seat, Gabbie looked up into the formidable face of Michael Nikolaides. He was regarding her so intently, it momentarily robbed her of the power to think with even an iota of clarity. It was an uncomfortable experience, one she was not used to, and with an effort she collected her scattered wits together.

'The weather in Crete,' she heard herself muttering.

Michael drew up a chair and sat down between his father and Gabbie, pouring himself a glass of wine from the carafe on the table. 'The weather in Crete is always warm,' he said, 'like the people. Warm, generous and easygoing.'

'Like you!' murmured Gabbie, recovered enough now to insert just the merest touch of acerbity into her voice.

'Like me,' he confirmed immodestly, and broke into a great roaring laugh like his father.

Much against her will Gabbie stared, fascinated by the great expanse of gleaming white teeth and sparkling eyes, black and wicked. His laugh transformed him from formidable into a dark virile man oozing self-confidence and charm. Gabbie hardened her heart, remembering how rude he had been at the interview, but it was easy to see that if he chose to, he would be able to charm the birds from the trees! All except this bird, she thought.

'What a pity Michael will not be in Crete to show you around,' said his father. 'You could do with a guide.'

Before Gabbie could open her mouth to reply, Michael cut in crisply. 'Oh, I don't know,' he said, 'she seems a very capable young woman, able to handle any situation. Isn't that what you said?' The laughter left his eyes and he stared intently at her again.

'I most certainly did say that,' replied Gabbie coldly, the look in his eyes sent an inexplicable shiver down her spine. 'And anyway, I hate guided tours!'

CHAPTER TWO

THE VERY next day after her meeting with Dr
Paulos, Gabbie rang her mother, asking if it would
be convenient for her to drive down and see her, to
say goodbye. For once her mother had sounded
quite enthusiastic on the phone.

'It will do you good, darling,' she said, 'going to
another country. Get you away from Peter and his
problems.'

'That's not the reason,' said Gabbie, springing to
the defence of her brother. 'In fact, if there was
anything I could do I'd stay.'

'Take my word for it, there isn't.' Was it her
imagination or had her mother's voice hardened?
'Let them get on with it, my dear—but there is
something you can do for me. I'll tell you about it
when you come down. I'm looking forward to your
visit—I do miss you, Gabbie, you know that, don't
you?'

For the first time in many years Gabbie felt a
surge of love for her mother, and wondered
whether she should be leaving England, but then
common sense told her Crete wasn't so far away.
Anyway, the drive down to Truro did more than
reinforce her feeling that she had done the right
thing; the weather was abysmal, it rained and
rained, the way it only can in England, thought

Gabbie. Cold, wet, driving rain, and the car plunged on through puddles that were in imminent danger of becoming mini-floods, until eventually she reached her destination; her mother's rather forbidding grey stone house on the outskirts of Truro. Normally in early summer, with pink and red rambling roses climbing the stone walls it looked less forbidding, but that day it looked cold and gloomy. The roses were all still in tight bud, clinging for dear life against the walls, the wind threatening their tenuous hold. Her mother, for once, had actually cancelled a case conference and was waiting at the house ready for her.

'I've got a hot meal ready,' she said as soon as Gabbie arrived. 'Change into something comfortable and come down into the kitchen, it's the only warm place in the house when the wind is blowing from the north-east!'

For some strange reason Gabbie felt vaguely uncomfortable. It was strange for her mother to be so well organised and thoughtful, almost purposeful. She changed into a sweater and dry jeans and joined her mother in the kitchen; it *was* the only warm place, her bedroom was freezing, the poor windblown rosebuds tapping frantically at the windowpane, as if asking to be let in.

'Sit down,' said her mother briskly, pouring out two glasses of sherry and passing one to her. She took a sip of her own, and looked at Gabbie. 'I have something to tell you.'

Gabbie did as she was told, looking at her mother through narrowed eyes. They had never been very close, sometimes she had even thought that if she hadn't bothered to keep in touch, her mother would have forgotten about her existence altogether. 'You sound very mysterious,' she commented.

'Nothing particularly mysterious,' her mother replied abruptly, turning away to fill two bowls with hot soup. Then placing them on the table, she took her place opposite her daughter. She was an older version of Gabbie, tall and slender with a boyish figure, her once fair hair now streaked with grey, but still elegant.

'I'm divorcing your father,' she said, 'on grounds of cruelty. My solicitor assures me that if I do it that way I shall get a sizeable portion of his estate. You know, of course, that he's just had a best-seller serialised for television.'

'Well, yes, but . . .' Gabbie wasn't surprised about the divorce, but on grounds of cruelty—that did surprise her. They had both been to blame, neither being really cruel, just thoughtless, and she was about to voice her thoughts when her mother interrupted.

'I shall want you to give evidence of cruelty—the way he left, how upset I was, how upset you were. I want to get every penny I can out of him!' she added, a harsh venomous note making her voice strident.

Gabbie was silent, then slowly she laid down her soup spoon. 'I can't do that,' she said slowly, 'it wouldn't be the truth. Perhaps he did upset you once, but that was years ago, and you never tried to get him back. You were both too caught up with your own careers.'

'I know that,' her mother motioned impatiently with her immaculately manicured hands, 'but now he's a millionaire, I don't see why I shouldn't share in some of his fortune.'

Horrified, Gabbie stared at the woman in front of her. Could this really be her mother talking like this?—a hard, calculating woman, intent on milking the man she had once professed to love.

'No!' the word was torn from her lips. 'I hardly know my father, but I'll not be a party to you fleecing him. You said Peter and Sue must get on with it—well, so must you.' She stood up abruptly, her chair scraping across the stone-flagged floor of the kitchen. 'Perhaps I'd better leave,' she said miserably, 'if that's all you want from me.'

Slamming her soup spoon down, her mother stood too. 'Perhaps you had,' she said coldly. 'I had expected a little more loyalty from my own daughter. After all, I was the one lumbered with you both when your father went off gallivanting all around the world!'

'Lumbered!' Gabbie cried out the word. 'Lumbered! Is that what you call having children?' She felt the tears welling up in her eyes. 'If there's one thing you've done for me, Mother, it's made me determined never to marry. I don't want to grow up into a bitter and twisted woman whose only thought in life is money!'

Her mother shrugged. 'Everyone needs money, my dear, but you can do without love. You'll find that out as you get older.'

'I already have,' retorted Gabbie bitterly, 'and the answer to your request is a positive, definite no. Divorce him if you want, but don't ask me to give evidence. I won't have anything to do with it!'

The kitchen door slammed behind her as she raced out and up the stairs to her bedroom, throwing her belongings back into her suitcase with a wild haste. She had to get out, back to London; she couldn't stay here. Her mother had finally destroyed the last slender threads of affection she had ever felt.

On the drive back to London she had cried half the way, and then a sort of dried-up coldness took over. She was glad she was going to Crete, and what was more, she *would* find a way to help Peter and Sue. They were *not* going to end up embittered individuals, hating each other, not if she could do something about it. She decided Dr Paulos might be able to help, he was a man of sensitivity and kindness; when she had settled in at the Institute she'd ask him. If anyone could give good advice, it would be him.

It was with a feeling of intense relief that Gabbie finally saw her suitcases disappear at the check-in desk at Gatwick and boarded the flight for Heraklion. As the plane taxied for take-off she looked out of the porthole, where grey skies overhead and rain-lashed runways greeted her gaze.

'I can't wait for the sunshine,' said the woman sitting next to her.

Gabbie turned and suddenly smiled. 'Neither can I,' she said with heartfelt conviction.

Even so, she was unprepared for the solid white glare of heat that blazed down from a brilliant blue sky. It was midday when they landed, and a car from the Institute was waiting for her when she emerged from the airport buildings at Heraklion. As it whisked her along the winding coast road to Aghios Nikolaos, Gabbie looked around her. Snow-white buildings slumbered in the heat of the noonday sun, their shutters drawn against the heat, brilliant purple bougainvillea festooning the walls. Hedges of wild geraniums blazed with colour, providing a fiery backdrop to the grey mountains towering up leaning inland, away from the brilliant blue of the sea.

After the cold grey wetness of England, it seemed to Gabbie that in a few short hours she had been transported to paradise; for a few fleeting seconds a mental picture flickered before her eyes of her mother's forbidding stone house in Truro, then resolutely she shut it out. This wasn't the place for unhappy memories. Already she had the feeling she could help her brother. She would invite both him and Sue out, perhaps in the sunshine everything would seem different and they would be able to talk to each other properly. The warmth of the sun certainly made her feel different; she felt she could cope with anything.

On arrival at the Institute she had expected to be driven to the nurses' quarters, but the driver took her to the large villa next door, which stood apart from the Institute set in its own grounds.

'You stay here,' he said in answer to her puzzled expression.

'But . . .' Gabbie was about to tell him he must have made a mistake.

'Gabbie, my dear, you've arrived at last! I waited for you, hoping we could have lunch together before I started this afternoon's clinic.' Dr Paulos came down the white marble steps, his hands held out in greeting. 'Come inside and eat, the whole family is waiting for you. We'll show you your room later.'

'The whole family?' exclaimed Gabbie. She thought he had told her Michael was their only son; surely he couldn't be here? He should be in Denver, Colorado, several thousand miles away.

With Dr Paulos still holding her hand, she was led through a cool hallway, pots of ferns standing on the chequered black and white marbled floor, through a series of rooms all painted white and decorated simply with expensive tapestries and large Chinese vases filled with hibiscus and mimosa, out on to a vine-shaded patio. Sitting beside a table, laid with a snowy white cloth on which stood a jug of fruit juice topped up with ice cubes, a tray of glasses by the side, was a small, plump dark woman, and the large, unmistakable form of Michael Nikolaides.

The woman stood up. 'I am Maria,' she announced in English, but with a heavy Greek accent, 'Dr Paulos' wife, and I shall be like your Greek mother!'

'Miss Kempson doesn't need a mother, she's quite a big girl!' The deep voice Gabbie had come to loathe during the interview in London cut in sharply.

'It will be lovely having a Greek mother,' corrected Gabbie, ignoring Michael, and smiling into the woman's sparkling brown eyes. 'It's very kind of you to have me to stay here until I find somewhere else.'

'Somewhere else?' Maria Nikolaides bounced back into her seat and began pouring out the ice-cold fruit juice. 'With Michael gone I shall need someone to look after, there's no hurry to find anywhere else.'

'Oh, you *are* going, then?' Gabbie turned and regarded the man in question coolly. To her intense annoyance she saw his swarthy face was a mask of amused malice; he was very well aware that she was not exactly pleased to see him there. 'I thought you'd already be in America,' she snapped.

Flipping the handles on the edge of his chair, he tipped it back, stretched out his enormously long legs and regarded her through narrowed black slitted eyes. 'I should have been, but there was a slight technical hitch at the last minute.'

Maria plumped up the cushions on the chair next to her, indicating that Gabbie should sit there. 'Isn't it lovely, dear, Michael will be able to show you around before he goes.'

'Well, actually,' Gabbie tried to phrase it tactfully; the last thing on earth she wanted was to be shown around, as Maria put it, but she didn't want to hurt her feelings, whatever she might feel about her son, 'I don't want to look around just yet, I'll leave sightseeing until later.'

'The hospital, not the island,' said Michael, banging the handles of his chair and sitting upright with one quick movement. 'You've come here to work, not for a holiday!'

A hot, painful flush spread across her face. What a fool she was—she had played right into his hands and he was enjoying every minute of her discomfiture. Crossly she glowered at him. 'I'm well aware of the reason I came,' she said, keeping her voice politely level with a great effort. 'I'm sorry if I misunderstood, but it's just that I thought your father would show me around as you weren't going to be working here.'

'You'll have the pleasure of my company for another week,' he said, jiggling the ice cubes round in his glass in a maddening way. 'It will take the load from my father if I show you what is expected of you, now that you're here.'

Gabbie contented herself with a demure, 'Of course,' as she took her fruit juice from Maria, and surreptitiously manoeuvred herself so that she was half turned away from Michael, towards Dr Paulos and his wife, the beaming motherly Maria. The faint snort of derision behind her told her that her unobtrusive move hadn't gone unnoticed! Oh, for one week's time, when the wretched man really would depart for Denver—it couldn't come soon enough, thought Gabbie. She looked out across the flower-filled garden, with the swimming pool and fountain at the end. It really was like paradise, even complete with its own serpent, she thought ruefully, painfully aware of the man just out of her vision.

Paulos and Maria wouldn't hear of her setting foot in the actual Institute until the next day, and after a light lunch Maria took her up to her room, a large airy room on the side of the villa overlooking the swimming pool.

'Now you must rest,' she said firmly, ignoring Gabbie's protestations that she didn't feel at all tired. 'Everyone has a sleep in the afternoons.'

'Everyone?' queried Gabbie, smiling. 'I can't imagine the work of the Institute stopping!'

Maria laughed, an infectious rumble of a laugh —a mini-version of her son's, thought Gabbie with a stab of surprise. 'No, not the Institute,' she agreed, 'although most of the patients snooze through the heat of the afternoon, and even Paulos does when he gets the chance, but never Michael.' She sighed heavily. 'Michael never relaxes properly.'

Gabbie slid her a sideways glance, thinking how well Maria's remark fitted in with her own impression of Michael Nikolaides. It was difficult to imagine him relaxing, he seemed to be permanently on the simmer, like some volcano about to erupt. It must be that aura emanating from him that made her feel edgy in his company, that and the fact that she disliked him for his sharp tongue. 'Perhaps he's just one of life's naturally energetic people,' she remarked, feeling she had to say something as

Maria was looking at her expectantly.

'Oh no,' Maria threw up her hands in a dramatic expression, 'he is restless. What he needs is a really good woman and a family. At thirty-seven he should be married.'

Gabbie laughed. The way Maria had said thirty-seven indicated that she thought it was something approaching ninety-seven! 'I'm sure he'll marry when he finds the right girl,' she said politely, thinking she pitied the poor female who ended up with that arrogant brute! She could just imagine the sort of husband he would be, demanding, over-bearing and above all possessive; it was illogical of her to think that, she knew, but all the same she just felt sure that was the way he would be.

'Are you married?' asked Maria, pausing in the doorway and looking at Gabbie speculatively.

'Not at the moment,' said Gabbie, adding for good measure, 'but there is someone special in England, so perhaps, who knows!'

It was wicked of her to manufacture a boyfriend who didn't exist, but at least that would stop Maria matchmaking. After all, she could hardly tell Michael Nikolaides' mother that she wouldn't marry her son if he was the last available man left on earth! Or indeed, that she had no intention of ever marrying anyway. One glance at the obviously happy relationship between Paulos and Maria had told her that the sort of fraught background she had come from would be totally incomprehensible to the Greek woman.

Maria nodded and smiled, then left the room;

Gabbie let out a long-drawn-out sigh of relief,
blessing her quick thinking for getting her off the
potential hook. She looked around. The room was
cool and the windows wide open, but shaded by the
slightly pulled shutters. Her suitcases stood piled in
the middle of the tiled floor. But Gabbie didn't feel
like unpacking; in spite of saying she didn't feel
tired, she found the unaccustomed heat making her
eyelids droop. She decided to have a short rest and
unpack later. Today was a sort of mini-holiday
after all, in spite of Michael's mocking remark
earlier about her having come to work, not for a
holiday!

With a swift decisive movement she slipped off
her dress and slip, then her tights, until she was
wearing only her brief panties and bra; thinking
that obviously her mode of dress would have to be
modified for life in Crete—no tights for a start, it
was far too hot. Pulling back the single snow-white
crocheted cotton coverlet, she was about to lie
down on the cool inviting sheets when a sound
beneath her room caught her attention. Curious,
she went across to the window, and pushing at the
green-painted shutters leaned out.

Below her, Michael Nikolaides walked across
the black and white marble tiles that edged the
entire villa, a brilliant yellow towel slung over his
naked, tanned shoulders. For a split second Gabbie
thought he was completely nude, then she saw he
was wearing just the briefest of black swimming
trunks. Against her will, her eyes were riveted on
the smooth copper of his skin, noting the way the

corded muscles of his thighs melted into his hip-
bones, then followed the curve round to his small,
tightly muscled buttocks. His stomach was flat, and
his narrow hips contrasted with the broad span of
his shoulders, and as he turned slightly Gabbie saw
that his massive chest was covered with a fine mass
of curly black hair. The muscles in her throat
constricted for a moment. He really was the sexiest-
looking man she had ever seen, and all her feminine
reflexes reacted.

Annoyed at her involuntary reaction, she made
to draw back and close the shutters, but Michael
must have seen the slight movement, because he
looked up, his dark gaze capturing hers and holding
it. 'Don't close the shutter on my account.' His
voice was mockingly sensual as deliberately he let
his eyes wander downwards.

With a gasp, Gabbie realised that she had next to
nothing on, and that the window sill only came to
her knees. Involuntarily she clasped one hand defensively across her breasts, and to her fury heard
him laugh outright. With a bang she pulled the
shutters close, and retreating back into the room,
flung herself crossly on the bed. Moments ago she'd
been sleepy, now she felt wide awake, and the
sound of Michael splashing vigorously as he swam
up and down the pool didn't help!

In order to stop her rebellious thoughts imagin-
ing that copper-bronzed body glistening with
water, she picked up a magazine lying on the bedside
table and started thumbing furiously through it.
The sooner Michael Nikolaides got to Denver the

better, she thought, feeling her rage towards him mount with every splash that echoed from the pool!

She awoke to silence, except for the chirruping of the cicadas. The magazine had slid to the floor, and a glance at her watch told her that she had actually been sound asleep for two whole hours. A feeling of almost ridiculous overwhelming relief surged over her. It had all been her over-active imagination. Michael Nikolaides might look sexy, but he hadn't disturbed her at all! It would take a lot more that some Greek glamour boy to distract her, she told herself, feeling a little smug.

Glorying in the coolness of a shower before she dressed, Gabbie hummed tunelessly but happily to herself, glad that all the hard work since the age of sixteen at proving to herself that she was immune to the male of the species hadn't even been dented! Although for one awful moment a couple of hours ago, she could have sworn it had; however, she did allow herself to acknowledge that she would have to be careful; any weakness had to be dealt with very firmly and doused. As if to prove her point, she turned the shower on extra cold, until she had to step out shivering.

That evening, she dined late with Dr Paulos and Maria, Michael was nowhere to be seen—working in the Institute, Paulos told her, as he topped up her wine glass. Later, in spite of her sleep that afternoon, she found she was ready for bed quite early, two glasses of strong red wine having made their effect.

'What time do I have to report for duty in the morning?' she asked, before taking her leave of Paulos, as he now insisted on her calling him, and Maria.

'Six o'clock.' Paulos sounded apologetic. 'I know it's earlier than in England, but here we start earlier and try to finish earlier on account of the heat. It is much better for the patients.'

She was told the maid, Katy, would be up and give her breakfast on the patio at a quarter to six, then all she had to do was to walk across to the main hall of the Institute and wait, just inside the front entrance, to be shown around. As she set her alarm clock for five o'clock, Gabbie hoped that perhaps it would be Paulos who would show her round the next day and tell her what needed to be done, but had an ominous feeling it would be the son, not the father.

Next morning she dressed in the crisp white uniform provided by the Institute, her waist cinched in with her navy belt fastened with the traditional silver buckle, the one she had bought when she had first qualified. As it was warm, even that early in the morning, she had forgone tights and slipped her feet into a pair of white lace-up canvas shoes, also provided courtesy of the Institute. Then she had partaken of a hasty breakfast, coffee and rolls alone on the patio, before setting off for the Institute.

She made her way across the still lawns, the dew still sparkling in the sunlight on the brilliant red of the hibiscus flowers which intermingled with

oleander bushes around the villa. On arrival at the
Institute, she stood waiting a little apprehensively
in the cool, tiled entrance hall.

Sounds of early morning activity echoed up and
down the corridors—babies crying, children's
voices murmuring, some laughing and chattering,
obviously all awake and waiting for their break-
fasts. She smiled at the sound of an extra boisterous
laugh. That was a child obviously well on the way to
recovery; there was nothing she liked more than
the sound of happy children.

'You look very cheerful.' Michael came out of a
door opposite from where she was standing.

Without thinking, and without selfconscious-
ness, Gabbie laughed. 'It's the children,' she told
him. 'Listen to that one laughing—I was just thinking that there can't be much wrong with him!'

Michael smiled back at her, his eyes crinkling at
the corners as he came towards her. 'You should do
that more often,' he said. 'Smile, I mean. And no,
there isn't much wrong with Thanos, in fact he's
going home today, which is probably what all the
noise is about.'

He placed a hand beneath her elbow and began
to steer her down the corridor in the direction of the
laughter. 'What's been wrong with Thanos?' enquired Gabbie, trying to ignore the huge brown
hand under her elbow, and the sudden rush of irritating pins and needles that swept through the
entire length of her body. Impulsively she wrenched
her elbow away, and Michael turned towards her,
raising a dark brow in a quizzical question mark.

'I think your thumb was on one of my nerves,' she heard herself mumbling. 'I have a sensitive elbow.'

'Well, I must say it's nice to know something about you is sensitive!' came the crushingly sarcastic reply.

Damn the man, but I asked for that, thought Gabbie, furious with herself for blurting out such a feeble remark, and wondering why it was, that although the corridor was reasonably wide, she should have such an overwhelming feeling of claustrophobia. He was much too close, hemming her in; she had an almost irresistible urge to flatten herself against the wall.

'Come and meet Thanos,' invited Michael, pushing open the door to the room, from which came much giggling and laughter.

A small boy sat on the bed, his leg encased in a full leg plaster cast, on which he was busily drawing butterflies with a brilliant green felt-tipped pen. The cause of the laughter and giggling was the fact that the nurse, a short dark girl, was endeavouring unsuccessfully to retrieve the pen.

'Good morning, Sophie, still having trouble with our patient, I see.' Michael spoke in English, Gabbie supposed for her benefit.

Sophie, the nurse in question, turned, and her face flushed bright pink when she saw the tall figure of Gabbie standing beside Michael. 'Oh, Dr Michael,' she exclaimed, making one last vain swipe at the pen, which Thanos adroitly whipped away, 'I wanted to send him home with a clean plaster!'

Gabbie laughed. 'Why bother?' she said. 'If I know anything about children, by the time he comes back to have it removed, it will be black, and covered with more scribblings anyway.' She stepped forward and held out her hand towards the dark girl. 'I'm Gabbie Kempson, from England.'

'Sophie Androutsopoulos,' the other girl replied a little shyly. But her twinkling eyes belied the shyness of her voice. She looked fun, Gabbie thought, not at all the shrinking violet she sounded!

'Miss Kempson is the new Sister from England engaged by my father. She will be organising special courses in paediatric nursing for all the nurses of the Institute.'

Gabbie turned in surprise and looked at Michael. Paulos had been very vague about her actual duties, and she had assumed she would just be doing a normal Sister's job. Organising teaching courses hadn't been mentioned, and for a second a lump of panic rose in her throat. She had never actually formally taught before, plenty of practical demonstrations as she had worked with the junior nurses watching, but never formal teaching.

Michael immediately noticed her surprised expression, because he murmured under his breath, 'We'll go into the details later,' before turning back to Thanos, who had put his pen away and was sitting up looking expectant. Michael wiggled the little boy's toes and said something in rapid Greek. Thanos nodded, and giggled again, then turned his big dark eyes, fringed with enormously long lashes, in the direction of Gabbie.

'*Kalimera*,' he said, beaming from ear to ear.

'*Kalimera*,' replied Gabbie, wishing she could speak Greek, and determining to try and master some as soon as possible. But thank goodness Paulos had said all the nurses spoke reasonable English. 'What type of fracture did he sustain?' she asked, looking at Sophie.

'A *fracture de ski*?' Sophie hesitated, and looked towards Michael for help. Gabbie looked puzzled, and also looked towards Michael, who was flicking through Thanos' notes on the clipboard at the end of the bed.

'A new term to you?' There was a sarcastic edge to his voice that made Gabbie want to throw something at him. He stood smiling at her, like some dark villain from a film, she thought mutinously. She knew what a *fracture de ski* was, but was uncertain that Sophie had got it right, and knew Sophie was uncertain too, so she said nothing, not wanting to embarrass the girl.

'This bright little lad managed to fracture both his tibia and fibula—he got the sort of fracture one usually only gets from a skiing accident, except he managed it by falling from his bicycle.' Michael tousled the little boy's dark curls affectionately, 'and now he's going home to pester his mother until it's time for the plaster to come off.'

'I see,' said Gabbie, in the most officiously

clipped toned of voice she could muster. There was really no need for him to throw some sarcastic remark at her whenever he got the chance! Glowering at his broad shoulders, she followed him from the room.

He had swept out without another word, obviously expecting her to follow, and then he took her on a lightning tour of the rest of the Institute. It was a long, low L-shaped building, rooms, sometimes single, sometimes for two or three beds, all opening off from one long single corridor that formed the main leg of the L-shape. Around the corner there were two operating theatres, and a small intensive care unit with just two beds, and at the far end of the building there were some steps, as the last part became two storeys.

'Rooms where we put patients in need of isolation, or parents who need to stay overnight,' said Michael briefly, waving in the direction of the steps. 'Now I'll show you your office and classroom.'

Oh dear, thought Gabbie at the mention of teaching, but she smiled brightly and merely said, 'Yes, that would be nice.' As she followed behind, overshadowed by the huge masculine form in front of her, she thanked her lucky stars she had brought a good number of paediatric books with her. If it meant that she had to sit up into the wee small hours, she'd present a teaching timetable for the Institute if that was what they needed.

'You have taught formally before?' asked Michael, uncannily reading her thoughts as he threw open a door and ushered her into a light and airy classroom. It overlooked the vegetables at the back of the Institute.

Deciding honesty was the best policy, Gabbie answered truthfully. 'No, actually I haven't, but I'm sure . . .'

'Oh yes, I forgot, you're trained to deal with any eventuality!' interrupted Michael, quoting the words she had used during the interview in London. A scathing glance raked her from top to toe.

Gritting her teeth, Gabbie determinedly outstared him. 'You don't approve of my appointment, do you?' she challenged.

He stepped towards her, and in spite of wishing she could run away Gabbie stood her ground, her sapphire eyes blazing. But even so it was almost impossible to ignore the trembling his nearness evoked.

'No, I don't,' he agreed. 'I wanted an older, more sensible woman, not one who's going to go dashing off and get married to the first man who asks her.'

'I've no intention of marrying anyone,' snapped Gabbie, 'ever!'

For an answer he put one long, tanned finger under her chin, and with deliberate force tipped her head slowly back. For a moment Gabbie felt as if she was drowning, as the dark pools of his eyes seemed to swallow her up.

'They all say that,' he said softly, with a cynical laugh, and then, to her outrage, kissed her full on the mouth.

CHAPTER THREE

'YOUR office is here,' said Michael casually, stepping away and completely ignoring the fact that he had just kissed her. It might never have happened, in fact Gabbie was so startled she wondered if indeed it had.

He pushed open a door leading off the classroom, then turned on his heel and left. 'I'll leave you to get organised. Perhaps we could go over the teaching rota this afternoon.' This last remark was flung over his shoulder as he departed.

'Tomorrow morning will be more convenient.' To her surprise Gabbie heard her voice ringing firm and clear, even though she felt as if she had just been clouted with a sledgehammer; she was startled and not a little annoyed at his arrogant, presumptuous attitude. 'I shall need a full list of the nurses, *and* I shall need to know their degree of experience before I can draw up a really meaningful rota.'

'It's on your desk, but tomorrow morning will do if you insist.' He stopped, then turned and looked at her. 'Sorry if I surprised you,' he said, his mouth twisting into a wide smile, 'but it was too good an opportunity to pass over.' He may have *said* sorry, but there was nothing repentant about his tone or expression!

'Next time try a little self-control.' Gabbie's voice was a shower of icicles as she tried to contain her mounting fury. The fury was partly directed at herself for allowing herself to be manoeuvred into such a ridiculous situation. She should have guessed he was a wolf, it was written all over him, only she had not taken it in; probably disappointed I didn't swoon into his arms right there and then, she snorted crossly to herself, once Michael had disappeared.

But there was no time to linger on time-wasting thoughts, she had the teaching rota to organise, and she was determined it would be faultless. Although no doubt the son of the Medical Director would find something to criticise!

After sorting out the list of nurses into three groups, she took time to wander round the Institute and meet as many of them as possible, telling them she would be organising regular seminars on paediatric nursing, but also making a point of telling them to call her if ever they needed help. She had no intention of becoming a purely academic nurse, she loved the practical side of nursing far too much for that.

At lunchtime the door to her office burst open after a brief knock, and a man she hadn't met before burst in. He was tall, with a shock of fair hair, gleaming even teeth and a big wide grin.

'Hi, Gabbie,' he said.

She grinned back; his expression was infectious. 'Don't tell me, let me guess—you must be Dr Jones, Paulos' American assistant.'

'Sam to my friends,' he said, perching on the edge of her desk and swinging one long leg. 'I've come to take you to lunch, to tell you what a terrific guy I am, and how I've been waiting with bated breath for your arrival ever since Paulos told me you were coming!'

Gabbie laughed delightedly; she liked Sam immediately. What a refreshing change from the oppressive Michael Nikolaides! 'What have you heard about me?' she parried, pushing the paperwork away. 'All good, I hope.'

'Oh,' said Sam, grinning widely, 'that you were a sweet young thing, desperately in need of affection and protection, and that I'm the best man to give it to you.'

'Are you always like this?' asked Gabbie as they walked down the corridor towards the *kafénion* which served as the staff canteen.

'Always,' he assured her, plucking a red rose from a vase of flowers on the windowsill and solemnly presenting her with it.

Sophie Androutsopolous whizzed past them, a tray of blood samples in her hands. 'Watch him,' she warned, 'he has a terrible reputation!' But it was said in an affectionate tone of voice. Obviously she liked him, and also obviously neither she nor any of the other girls took Sam very seriously, and Gabbie could well imagine why.

Over lunch he filled her in on the background of the Institute, founded by Paulos with his own money after the war, and then helped by the government with small grants, although most of the money still came from private means.

'Do you manage to treat everyone who needs it?' asked Gabbie. 'It seems such a small hospital.'

'Of course a lot slip through the net,' admitted Sam, 'especially in the mountain villages. The people there tend not to trust towns and the sterile cleanliness of the Institute. So we hold regular clinics in the actual villages, and as well as treatment give basic health education. The most common thing we treat amongst the children is chest ailments.'

'What, here?' asked Gabbie in surprise. 'As it's so warm I thought . . .'

'It's not so warm in the mountains, especially in winter when it snows up there. Although never down here on the coast,' replied Sam, smiling at her surprise. 'But if you can teach these girls good paediatric care, and don't worry, if it's too sophisticated, they can always scale it down, then we can send them out to the villages on their own.'

Gabbie nodded. 'I see—a bit like the health visitors we have back in England.'

'Yes,' said Sam.

'Although I don't think Dr Michael Nikolaides would approve if I taught them anything too sophisticated, he was pretty scathing about my own ability to deal with emergencies without hi-tech equipment.'

'Don't worry about him,' said Sam with a dismissive wave of his hand. 'He's a born misogynist, bound to disapprove. If he'd had his way you'd never have been appointed.'

'So he's already told me,' said Gabbie wryly, 'but I wouldn't have thought he was a misogynist, more likely a womaniser!'

'It's possible to be both,' Sam observed shrewdly. 'I might love 'em and leave 'em, but at least I *do* love them. He . . .' he stopped mid-sentence as the tall form of Michael wended its way through the now crowded tables of the small *kafénion* and came towards them.

'I see you've met Sam,' he said, then looked pointedly at his watch.

Sam laughed and draining the last dregs of his coffee stood up. 'Gee, Michael, you'll go down well in the States—they're all workaholics there!' He clasped a friendly hand on his colleague's shoulder. 'You don't have to remind me, I know I have two orthopaedic cases scheduled for theatre and I'm just about to go.'

'Dr Stergis will probably have the first one already asleep,' said Michael, but he was grinning back goodnaturedly at Sam. The two men evidently got on well together, in spite of their completely different approach to work.

Sam sighed. 'Yeah, since he qualified in anaesthesia, he's so keen, if I'm not careful one of these days he'll put me to sleep!' He waved goodbye Gabbie and left the *kafénion*.

Gabbie too drained her coffee cup. 'I must get back to my rotas,' she said, standing up quickly. The last thing she wanted was for Michael to think she took too long for lunch!

'Ah yes, how are they going?'

'You'll have them tomorrow morning, and then you can judge,' replied Gabbie firmly.

'Did you like Sam?'

The question surprised her. 'Er . . . yes, he's very friendly. Very open, typically American, I'd say. I think I'll get on very well with him,' she finished.

'Hmm . . .' an enigmatic murmur as he watched her from beneath half lowered lids was the only reply she got.

For some reason it unnerved her just as much as when they were arguing. 'I . . . I must get back to the rotas,' she repeated hurriedly, starting to move away.

Michael got up, stretching himself like a great lion. The chairs in the *kafénion* were really too small for him, thought Gabbie, watching, then he said, 'Yes, we'll do that tomorrow morning.' He walked with her to the doorway. 'Before I leave.'

'You're leaving tomorrow?'

He suddenly laughed, that great flashing, devastating laugh, that transformed him into the most attractive-looking creature on earth, Gabbie found herself thinking. 'Don't look so pleased about it,' he said.

After Michael's departure the next day, Gabbie found it easier to settle down. He had, much to her surprise, noted her schedule for teaching, nodding with approval at the way she had split the nurses into three groups, depending on their experience.

He had also approved of the various aspects she intended to teach.

'Good basic principles,' he had said. 'Child growth and development, principles of care in the newborn, infants and children, and the adolescent patient. Nothing too pie-in-the-sky.'

That was the nearest thing to a compliment she got, and Gabbie was pleased. She didn't tell him that was only the beginning, she had more complicated things planned for later, but later he wouldn't be there, he would have gone. She felt even happier when he had actually gone that afternoon. Now I can get down to the job in hand, she thought, with no one to annoy me, criticise or generally disturb me. Now that he had gone she let herself admit that there was something very disturbing about him, although she put it down to the fact that she had been constantly on edge, awaiting a flash of criticism. Knowing that he had disapproved of her appointment would have made life intolerable, if she had had to work with him, but thank goodness he was gone.

In the two weeks following his departure Gabbie forged a good working relationship with both Paulos and Sam, and to her pleasure found that the nurses didn't hesitate to ask for help when they had a particularly difficult case to deal with. She found her new role as a teacher rewarding, and at the same time got enough clinical contact with the children to keep her more than contented.

The Institute was very busy, and between them Paulos and Sam ran it extremely efficiently, keeping patients in the beds for as short a time as possible, so that their through-put was high. Then there were the large outpatient clinics they ran, both at the Institute and in the surrounding villages. As yet Gabbie hadn't managed to get out of the Institute to one of the village clinics, but she intended to as soon as possible.

On the Wednesday of her third week at the Institute, she took the most junior nurses for their afternoon seminar, and had chosen admission procedure to hospital as her subject. It hadn't been on her original schedule, but she'd noticed that some of the girls were, quite unintentionally, a little thoughtless, not giving the children the extra care needed to facilitate the adjustment needed to a hospital environment.

She regarded the group of upturned faces before her and smiled encouragingly. It was their first session with her, and she could see some of them were apprehensive. 'What I'm going to list for you to discuss is very basic,' she told them.' 'Perhaps you'll even think I'm being silly telling you these things, but they are an important part of the actual treatment.'

'Why do you say that, Miss Kempson?' That was Heleanna; she was always curious, always the first to ask the questions on the ward.

Gabbie smiled. 'Let me explain. When a child is admitted to hospital, a series of procedures should occur to help everyone—the child, his or her parents, and the hospital staff. First, obtain baseline data.'

The girls all studiously wrote in their study books, then looked up expectantly.

Gabbie went on to explain that although that sounded very grand, what it really meant was asking a series of questions in order to find out as much as possible about the child, his family and most particularly the child's individual needs.

'What do you mean, individual needs?' asked Heleanna.

'Does the child have any special likes or dislikes, does he take a special toy to bed, does he hate being in the dark? Those are the things you need to know. Can you imagine how frightening it must be to a small child—long white corridors, a strange room, strange people all dressed in white, and then perhaps being left alone in the dark at night. Especially if he or she always has a light at home and is frightened of the dark.'

'You mean we've got to try to make it as much like home as possible?'

Gabbie nodded. 'Yes, that's the most basic thing pertinent to a child, *and* his parents—we mustn't forget them. They can be just as worried, just as frightened.'

She handed out a stencilled questionnaire to all the girls, telling them that in future one should be filled out for each child on admission to the institute. 'These particular forms are in English,' she said, 'but Valissa, Dr Paulos' secretary, has said she will type them out in Greek if you prefer.'

To Gabbie's intense relief, all the girls had said they preferred to work in English. 'It will help our

English,' laughed Heleanna, the universal spokes-woman. 'I certainly intend to go there to work one day.' She looked at the form and started to read out loud. '(a) Routines at home including disciplinary actions, all the way down to (o) Is mother to be resident? A lot of questions,' she observed.

'Tell me, after you've given it a week's trial, whether or not you think any of them are un-necessary,' said Gabbie. 'And now we'll move on to the more clinical aspect of admission, and the equipment you *must* have ready before you ever set eyes on the child.' She ticked off the items on her fingers. 'Admission record card, scales, measuring rod for height, tape measure for head circumfer-ence, watch with second hand, stethoscope and sphygmomanometer, thermometer, oral or rectal according to age, and lubricant for rectal thermo-meter.' Handing round another sheet with the items listed, she told them that in future, a supply of such charts would be kept in each room, and should be checked off and inserted into the back of the notes on admission. 'That way we can all make sure we haven't missed anything,' she said.

She hoped the girls wouldn't take offence. The other nurses in the other groups had accepted her recommendations well, but record keeping was the one area in which she felt the Institute could do with a little shake-up, the attitude being rather hit-and-miss, which made it very difficult if a pa-tient needed to be re-admitted later.

'I'm sorry if you think I'm being ultra-fussy,' she said almost apologetically, 'but in the long run . . .'

'Oh no,' Ariana, one of the other girls, spoke this time, 'we all want the Kriti Institute to be as much like an English hospital as possible. We want it to be the best on the island!

Gabbie felt a warm glow. It was a pleasure to work with such enthusiastic nurses, and suddenly she realised how jaded she had actually become in England without ever realising it, always working under pressure, with the ever-present threat of closure of the hospital hanging over all the staff. From her personal point of view, perhaps the closure had been a good thing, she reflected; without the impetus necessitated of having to find another job, she would never have dreamed of coming to a place like Crete to work. Exchanging smiling goodbyes with the girls as they gathered together their papers and prepared to leave the seminar room, Gabbie felt that fate had been kind to her, propelling her unexpectedly in the right direction, working with two such easy going doctors as Paulos and Sam, in such a lovely place.

She was still smiling broadly, and preparing to walk through to her office, when the door to the seminar room burst open and a grim-faced Sam, followed by a tearful Maria, burst in. 'Paulos has been taken ill, up in a remote village on the Lassithi plateau,' he said, not bothering with preliminaries. 'Thank God the village priest had a telephone, so they could let us know. I'm going up there now with Spyros—he'll drive Paulos' car back, and I'll bring him back in the ambulance.'

'Taken ill? But what . . . ?'

'Sounds like a heart attack from the description Father Mothestos gave me,' replied Sam briefly. 'I'll leave you in charge of the Institute while I'm away—*and* Maria,' he added.

'But Sam, please let me come with you,' pleaded Maria, clutching at his arm.

'No,' said Sam, none too gently, 'it's better if I go alone.' He flashed Gabbie a mute 'help me' plea.

'It's better for Sam and Sypros to go alone,' said Gabbie gently, firmly prizing the clinging, tearful Maria from Sam's arm. 'It will be quicker, and we can stay here and get everything ready for Paulos' return.'

'Get the room next to Intensive Care ready,' said Sam. 'You know what to prepare.'

Gabbie nodded quickly. That meant just about everything; it might be a heart attack, but equally it could just as easily be something else. 'I'll leave nothing to chance,' she said.

'Good girl!' Sam was already out of the room and gone, leaving his words lingering on the air.

Maria sobbed noisily. 'Suppose he is dead, and I won't be there?' She wrung her hands in anguish.

'Now, Maria,' said Gabbie firmly, 'we've got to look on the bright side. The priest isn't a doctor, he could have easily misread the signs. The last thing we want is for Paulos to return and find you in this state. Then *he* would start worrying.' She took Maria's arm gently but very firmly. 'You come and help me get the room ready, and then we'll both have a coffee together while we're waiting for their return.'

By the time Sam arrived back with Paulos in the ambulance, Maria had calmed down, and the fact that her beloved husband was still very much alive, although quite plainly ill, made her rally round even more.

'What do you think?' asked Gabbie under her breath as she and Sam installed Paulos in the room she had prepared.

'A stroke,' said Sam. 'He was right-sided hemiplegia, but hasn't lost consciousness, thank God.'

It was an anxious night for all of them. Sam carefully monitored Paulos' condition, while Gabbie volunteered to sit up with him for half the night, knowing Sam had half a day's operating to perform next day, as well as an outpatients clinic. As she sat in the dimly lit room, watching Paulos, who was now sleeping, she wondered how on earth the clinic would manage. They had their Greek anaesthetist, Dr George Stergis, but Sam couldn't do everything else on his own; perhaps there would be someone in Heraklion who could help. The problem was that with a stroke one could never be certain of how long, or indeed even if a complete recovery would be made. Gabbie looked at the sleeping face of Paulos. It was unfair that a man who had given his entire life for others should be struck down; get well, she prayed silently, get well.

Next morning Paulos did seem better for his peaceful night's sleep, and Sam decided he would be better off back in his own villa than as a patient in the Institute. But first he made Maria promise not to fuss too much, but to leave Paulos quiet for at least the next week, and keep him on a very light diet. So Paulos was transferred, and Gabbie stayed with Maria for a while, showing her how the pillows should be kept low, and emphasising that peace and quiet were essential for his recovery. When she was satisfied that she had done as much as was humanly possible, she made her way back to the Institute and Sam's office.

For once Sam didn't look his usual bright, bouncing self. His fair hair fell over his forehead in a lank fringe, and his face was grey with tiredness. 'I've just called Michael,' he said with an air of resignation.

'Yes, of course,' said Gabbie. 'What did he say?'

'He's coming back immediately—there's no alternative. I can't get anyone else as good, and I can't run the Institute with just George Stergis.'

'Well, of course I realise you can't do that,' said Gabbie, 'but surely there must be someone else who could do the job until Paulos . . .'

'Paulos may never practise again,' said Sam, 'only please don't mention that fact to either him or Maria. Michael was right, he should have retired last year—he *is* seventy, you know. Even if he makes a complete recovery, the stress of the work-load of running this place would be too much for him. It needs a younger man, and Michael is the man.'

'Yes, I suppose so,' said Gabbie slowly. It was selfish of her, she knew, not wanting Michael Niko-laides to come back. He was probably the best man for the clinic, and the obvious choice to take over from his father. 'How does he feel about leaving his research?' she asked.

Sam grinned. 'You don't know Michael very well yet! People and patients come first, highest on his list of priorities. Research, as he's just said to me, can always be done by someone else. These are his people, he wants to care for them.'

'I can understand that,' said Gabbie. But all the same she viewed his imminent return with some dismay; she couldn't leave now the Institute needed her too, but working with the man who hadn't approved of her appointment wasn't going to be easy. However, she kept such disquieting thoughts to herself. Sam had plenty of other things to worry about, and a mountain of work to do until Michael returned.

Michael arrived back in Crete three days after his father's stroke. He looked tired and drawn from the long flight, and was obviously jet-lagged. Gabbie kept out of the way the evening of his arrival, leaving the family together; then from her room she saw the lights in Sam's office burning late into the night. Obviously he and Michael were planning their work-load.

Next morning she popped in as usual to see Paulos before she started work. He was speaking a little now and seemed rather agitated when she entered his room. With his left hand he beckoned Gabbie to come closer. 'You'll stay?' he whispered the words with difficulty.

Gabbie smiled reassuringly. He couldn't say it, but she knew he had felt the antipathy between herself and Michael, and was obviously worried that she would leave now that Michael would be running the Institute. 'Of course I'll stay,' she said, squeezing his hand. 'You didn't think I'd desert you, did you? Don't worry, everything will go just the way we planned it, and it won't be long before you'll be back there, taking your part.'

Paulos shook his head, but managed a lopsided smile. 'Stay,' he whispered urgently.

'I will, I promise. I'll stay as long as I'm wanted.'

'That might be for a very long time.' Unknown to her, Michael had quietly entered his father's room. He looked worried, but quickly switched to a confident smile as his father's eyes alighted on his face.

'Then in that case I'll stay for a very long time,' said Gabbie quietly, and with a final squeeze of Paulos' hand she left.

As she crossed in the early morning sunlight to walk towards the Institute, she knew she would have to move from the villa. She had committed herself to staying for as long as needed, and to do that she had to get on with Michael Nikolaides, and it wouldn't be easy working *and* living in the same house. The sensible thing to do would be to rent a little house of her own—she had seen one advertised in an agent's window only the other day when she had been on a shopping spree down into Aghios Nikolaos, and the rent had been very reasonable. From the photograph it had looked very picturesque, and it was only a few kilometres away, up in the next village. As soon as she had some free time that morning she telephoned the agent and made arrangements to rent the cottage, sending Spyros down with one month's rent in advance, so that he could bring the keys back; she could move in that night.

It had been her plan originally to pop out to inspect the cottage before actually committing herself, but it was impossible, the Institute was frantically busy, so she had taken the chance and sent Spyros down. Then, just to finish off the day, Sam asked if she would mind going to the village of Aghia Triada with Sophie, where, according to the schoolteacher, there was a severe outbreak of pediculosis amongst the children.

'If we don't nip it in the bud now,' he had said apologetically, after breaking the news to her, 'we'll have the whole village infested with secondary complications. You can run the clinic in the schoolroom there, the teacher has everything prepared, so all you need to do is take out the necessary equipment.'

Gabbie nodded. 'I must just speak to Maria first,' she said, wondering how she was going to tactfully announce that she would be moving out that night. In the event, she needn't have worried. Michael was nowhere to be seen when she dashed across to the villa at lunchtime, and Maria was so preoccupied with Paulos that Gabbie knew she was almost glad in a way. It was one less person for her to worry about.

'It *is* a good house?' Maria had asked when Gabbie had told her.

'It's lovely,' said Gabbie, 'and as soon as Paulos

is better, I want to entertain you both to dinner.'

Maria smiled a little wistfully. She had grown accustomed to the idea now that it would take a long time for her husband to recover. 'That won't be yet,' she said, 'but you will come and see us sometimes?'

'Every single day,' promised Gabbie. 'Now, I must rush, I'm being sent out into the field, so to speak, to Aghia Triada.' She kissed them both, and after grabbing a quick coffee and demolishing a Greek pastry dripping with honey and pistachio nuts, she set out with Sophie for the village in her rented Fiat Panda.

Gabbie was glad she had Sophie with her. Most of the children in the small village had become infected, even the daughter of the richest man in the village, much to his horror. The parents had gathered anxiously with their children, after being called to the school by the teacher, who had first become aware of the problem. Gabbie hastened to instruct Sophie to explain that head-lice were no respecters of persons, and it only needed one to start off an epidemic.

'Please be tactful,' said Gabbie. 'Explain to them that it doesn't mean we think them dirty, but that every family must use the lotion we give them and wash all the bedlinen carefully as well as their heads.'

Sophie nodded, and proceeded to hand out small bottles of carbaryl lotion to the parents, instructing them on how to prevent re-infestation; while Gabbie applied the pediculicide lotion to the scalp and hair of the affected children, leaving it to dry naturally before then shampooing and combing while wet. Several of the children had secondary complications, eczema and impetigo, and she was thankful she had brought neomycin and hydrocortisone cream with her and was able to start the appropriate treatment on the spot.

By the time she and Sophie had finished they were exhausted, but before they left they reassured the families once more, telling them to call the Institute if they had any further worries. It was getting late and both girls were ready to drop. Sophie arranged to follow up with a visit the next week, just to make sure all was well, and that the treatment had worked.

'Do you ever have that in England?' asked Sophie, as Gabbie carefully drove the little car down the narrow winding road back to Aghios Nikolaos.

'Of course,' Gabbie chewed her lip as she swerved to avoid an extra large pothole before continuing with her answer, 'but in England we have school nurses, and other nurses in the community called health visitors, so it would be picked up before it got too bad.'

'Oh,' said Sophie, sounding relieved.

'Don't think the children here are the only ones to get nits,' said Gabbie with a smile. 'Children all over the world get them, and their mums and dads if they're not careful! It's very common.'

Sophie sat back and relaxed, pride satisfied, and Gabbie knew she'd been worried that the English nurse might be thinking badly of her fellow Greeks. She smiled to herself as she concentrated on the road once more, negotiating the series of hairpin bends that finally led one down to the Kriti Institute.

Once there, she dropped off Sophie and made her way back to the villa, blessing the fact that she had had the foresight to pack her suitcases that morning. She was so tired she only wanted to have a bath and drop into bed, but that would have to wait; she had to move first.

Following the directions sent up by the agent with the keys, she finally arrived at her very own villa, and taking one horrified look, realised she should have inspected it first! The house, or cottage as it should have been called, but referred to by the agent as a villa/cottage, stood alone on the side of the mountain, a good half mile at the very least from the nearest village. True, it did have a spectacular view of the mountains, and the smooth blue waters in the bay of Mirabello spread out below, but one wall was badly cracked and was propped up with a huge olive branch. The lavatory was a hundred yards down a stony path, and consisted of a small stone hut with a crude wooden box placed over a hole in the ground, and the supply of water, as far as Gabbie could see, had to be pumped up by hand from a well outside the kitchen door!

After the initial shock, Gabbie gritted her teeth resignedly, and telling herself that an outside loo and water from the well didn't matter in Crete where the sun always shone, determined to make the best of it. The crack in the wall looked as if it had been there for years, and hadn't penetrated through the thick walls to the inside, which at least was spotlessly clean, although the furniture was spartan. She had just unpacked two suitcases, and had chosen the bedroom which had the view over the sea, pausing for a moment to admire the view; the hillside still shimmering in the heat, even though it was evening, and the waters of the bay misting dark grape blue away into the distance. I'm going to *love* it here, she told herself firmly, going back to the car to get the other suitcase.

It was then she noticed the looming black cloud rolling rapidly across the sky from the mountain behind the little house. It would have been difficult not to have noticed it, because it spread with frightening speed across the entire vista, blotting out the warmth of the sun, and simultaneously a chill wind suddenly sprang up.

Hurriedly Gabbie dragged the suitcase, the heaviest one, from the car, and had just got it into the middle of the kitchen floor when it started to rain. Not driving, lashing rain as in England, but straight down, as if someone was emptying a bucket from on high.

The colour of the sky changed from blue to grey to black, and suddenly there was a flash of lightning followed immediately by a great clap of thunder. With a scream, the last of Gabbie's brave resolve disappeared, as she dissolved into tears of fright and tiredness, sitting hunched up on the suitcase. A second clap of thunder had her on her feet. The house had shaken, she was sure it had; at the same moment the huge figure of a man, a wet tarpaulin flapping around his shoulders, came through the open kitchen doorway, and Gabbie screamed again.

Then with a flood of relief she realised it was Michael Nikolaides. 'What the hell do you think you're doing in this place?' he demanded, discarding the tarpaulin and throwing it in the corner.

'I . . .' but before she could answer, lightning struck a stunted tree barely two hundred yards down the mountainside. With a gasp of terror, Gabbie threw herself towards Michael, to be gathered up in his large, strong arms.

'A bit different from England, eh?' his deep voice said against her hair.

Terrified, she could only nod in reply, keeping her eyes tightly shut. Suddenly his huge size didn't seem menacing at all, it was warm and comforting. Locked in the circle of his arms, she felt that nothing could get at her, not even if every thunderbolt in heaven was hurled at her.

CHAPTER FOUR

THE STORM abated with the same astonishing speed as it had begun, leaving everything dripping, torrents of water running down the mountainside in little streams. Ashamed at having given way to irrational fear, Gabbie pushed herself away from Michael.

'I'm sorry,' she muttered, 'I don't know what came over me. I'm not usually so weak at the knees.'

'Why apologise?' he enquired, a smile curving his lips. 'You *are* a woman, after all. All women need men, you are no different from any other.'

'I'm a *professional* woman,' said Gabbie, annoyed at his patronising tone of voice. 'If I hadn't been so dog-tired, I wouldn't have been worried at all! Surely even men must get a little worried sometimes?'

'Perhaps,' said Michael, wandering around the kitchen inspecting the bare contents with interest, as if he personally never envisaged getting nervous about anything. 'But not many men would sit weeping all alone on a suitcase in the middle of the floor, only to fling themselves into the arms of a complete stranger when he made an appearance!'

Gabbie flushed. Was that what he thought? That she'd fling herself at a complete stranger? 'If it had been a *complete* stranger I'd have hit him,' she said, her usual self-reliance beginning to reassert itself, 'but I knew it was you, although I will admit it did show a momentary weakness on my part,' she acknowledged as she started to drag the suitcase towards the stairs that led to the upper floor.

'Here, let me, for goodness' sake. The last thing I need is you away sick with a strained back!' Michael picked up the heavy suitcase as if it weighed a few ounces, and carried it up the stairs. 'Which room?' he asked briefly, pausing on the landing.

Silently Gabbie pointed to the room she had chosen as her bedroom, and he dumped the case by the side of the bed. 'A double bed, I see,' he said, a wicked expression suddenly sparkling in his eyes, looking at the bed and then back to Gabbie.

To her horror, she felt a panic-stricken flush spread across her face. He had the most uncanny knack of being able to unnerve her with just a few well-chosen words. 'Yes,' she said stiffly, wishing she could think of some crushing reply, and that he would go.

'Planning to share it with anyone in particular?'

He was insufferable! The flush deepened to crimson and before she could stop herself Gabbie heard her voice saying, sounding affectedly casual, 'I shall be inviting friends to stay.' She turned away abruptly and clattered down the stone stairs leading back to the kitchen.

'Male or female?' Michael followed her.

'Male.' That should shut him up, she thought, busying herself opening cupboard doors unnecessarily, wishing he would go.

'You surprise me.' He stood watching her, arms folded in a contemplative way. 'You gave me the impression of being an ice maiden, and you certainly told me you had no intention of marrying anyone.'

Gabbie swung round crossly. 'I *have* no intention of marrying, but that doesn't mean to say I can't have men friends. Anyway, you were the one who jumped to the conclusion that I'd be sharing the bed—I didn't mention it.'

'Ah,' said Michael, walking across towards her, 'you are an ice maiden after all.'

'I . . . I don't need men, if that's what you mean,' Gabbie found herself stammering almost defensively. She backed away, only to find the hard edge of the ancient stone sink digging into her back. 'In fact you could say I've learned not to trust men,' she blurted, and immediately regretted such an indiscreet remark.

'An ice maiden, just as I thought, but . . .' he put a finger to her lips to silence Gabbie, who had opened her mouth to protest, 'fire melts ice, you know, and I've always been considered fiery!'

'Not fiery enough for me,' she snapped. Great arrogant man, she had been right in her original estimation, he did think he was the answer to every maiden's prayer! 'Personally I don't find you attract me at all, so don't bother wasting your charm on me,' she added in her most freezing tone of voice.

Michael laughed. 'Don't worry, I wasn't going to bother. I prefer women who are soft and cuddly, women who look like women, not flat-chested boys!'

'Oh!' furiously Gabbie clenched her fists behind her back. He'd hit her where it hurt. She'd always been horribly selfconscious about her lack of bosom, not wishing for enormous boobs, but always longing for just a little more than the gentle swell of breasts she possessed. 'You're the rudest man I've ever met!' she spluttered angrily, wondering how on earth she was going to keep to her promise and stay working at the Institute for as long as she was needed.

Michael laughed, his great flashing laugh, his teeth gleaming whitely in the rapidly darkening gloom of the kitchen. He was completely unabashed. 'You know, I rather like you when you're angry,' he said, 'much better than when you're playing at the frigid ice maiden!'

'If you don't shut up,' shouted Gabbie, losing all self-control, 'I won't be responsible for my actions! I'll . . . I'll,' she picked up a heavy iron saucepan that looked as if it had been manufactured during the early Middle Ages, 'I'll hit you!'

Michael put his hands up in the air in a gesture of surrender. 'All right, all right, I'll be polite, only don't hit me with that or we'll need another Medical Director for the Institute!'

Shamefaced at her loss of temper, Gabbie lowered the saucepan. 'We need a light on,' she said. 'Where's the switch?'

'You don't really think this place has electricity, do you?

'Well . . . of course, I . . .' She stopped, horrified. Of course, she ought to have realised—outside loo, well water, why should she have thought such a thing as electricity would be laid on!

'That's why I originally came up here, not because of the storm. I didn't see how someone coming from the world of microwave ovens and push-button telephones could possibly manage up here! You didn't inspect this place first, did you?'

'No,' said Gabbie, her voice short with temper at herself for being so stupid, 'but now that I'm here I'm staying,' she added defiantly. 'It may not have all mod cons, but . . .'

'You can say that again,' grinned Michael, 'it hasn't got *any*.'

'But I shall manage,' continued Gabbie, ignoring his interruption. 'I chose this place because I like being alone—and there's no need for you to think I can't look after myself, because I can.' In spite of her defiant words, however, her heart was sinking lower and lower. Roughing it had never been one of her strong points. One week at a very wet and windy Girl Guides' camp, when she'd been younger, had convinced her that the back-to-nature life was not for her! Frantically she cast her mind back, wondering about oil lamps and things—how did one light them?

With uncanny perception Michael said, 'I'll just stay for a bit until you get the hang of things, as you seem determined to stay put. Here, hold this,' he thrust a lamp into Gabbie's hands, 'I'll show you how to light it.'

It was a Calor gas lamp, and in fact quite simple to use, Gabbie noticed with an immeasurable flood of relief. Once the soft light from the lamp flooded the kitchen, everything looked far less forbidding; it even gave the place a cosy look. Outside, the black thunderclouds had lingered on, so it had got dark much earlier than usual; and although Gabbie protested that she didn't need him, Michael insisted on staying, showing her how to use the Calor gas stove for cooking, and pumping up the water from the well into the water storage tank on top of the roof.

'The water's quite drinkable,' he said, as she experimentally turned on the tap. 'This cottage was lived in until two weeks ago. The owner has gone to London to work for a couple of years.'

'You knew the owner?' Gabbie was surprised.

'Yes, that's how I knew how basic the accommodation was when my mother gave me your address!' He grinned again, and in spite of herself, Gabbie found she was smiling back. 'Now I've done all the hard work, aren't you going to invite me to supper?' he asked.

Phrased like that, Gabbie didn't have much alternative, but to ask him to stay. 'Although it's going to be very simple,' she said, 'taramasalata and bread, then an omelette with peppers, but no wine—I forgot to get any.'

'One moment.' Michael disappeared and went back to his car, which Gabbie could see parked beside hers. Suddenly she was glad he was staying, although she would have died rather than have admitted it to him. But having someone else in the cottage for the first evening took away the feeling of uneasiness she'd first had when she'd seen how lonely and isolated it was.

The kitchen door opened, and a large bottle of red wine was unceremoniously thrust at her. 'A present,' said Michael, smiling and looking friendly. In fact the friendliest she had ever seen him look.

'Thank you,' said Gabbie, taking the wine and smiling a little uncertainly, not sure whether she liked the new friendly Michael Nikolaides. At least when they were at loggerheads, she knew precisely where she stood.

'You know what they say,' Michael said lightly, his eyes gleaming blackly in the lamplight, 'beware of Greeks bearing gifts!'

'I shall bear that in mind,' Gabbie told him, 'you may be sure of that.' Yes, and I better had, she told herself, acutely aware of Michael's presence, his tall frame dominating the room. She reminded herself that she didn't like him, and he certainly didn't like her—he hadn't approved of her appointment, and didn't even approve of her appearance; his remark about her being like a flat-chested boy still rankled. And yet he managed to evoke the most disturbing sensations of any man she had met. It's because you're so uncertain of him, she told herself firmly, cutting up the large crusty loaf she had brought with her. One minute he'll be friendly, the next he'll be scathing, there's always the danger of ending up with egg on your face if you're not constantly on guard!

But over supper she found her resolve to keep up her guard gradually dissolving, melting away in the face of Michael's disarmingly friendly conversation. Almost before she knew it, she had told him about her mother and father, and what her mother had asked her to do, now that her father had become famous.

'What did you say?' asked Michael sombrely, his eyes glinting as he looked at her over the rim of the tin mug serving as a wine glass.

'I refused to have anything to do with it,' said Gabbie sadly, remembering the last encounter with her mother. She was silent for a few moments; talking of her family had reminded her of her brother's marital problems, and she felt a guilty stab. She'd got so caught up and so involved with the Institute since she started working in Crete, she'd hardly given him a thought at all; now she had a sudden flash of inspiration. She would invite Peter to come and stay with her at the cottage, maybe then they could talk properly, and she would be able to help him sort things out. Yes, that was what she'd do—she'd phone him on Sunday, when the rates were cheaper, and ask him to come out.

Michael drained the last of his wine from the cup and looked at his watch. 'I'd better be going,' he said, 'if you're sure you'll be OK here all alone.'

'Of course I'm sure,' said Gabbie.

'And you're going to stay here for all the time you're at the Institute?' His voice sounded disbelieving as he looked around the bare kitchen.

'Definitely,' said Gabbie with far more determination than in fact she was actually feeling. 'It will be perfect—there's plenty of room. I can have friends to stay, in fact I've already decided on the first person I'm going to invite.' She was thinking of Peter as she spoke.

'Will the first be male or female?' asked Michael.

'Male,' said Gabbie, and was about to go on and explain that it would be her brother, but the words were lost as he interrupted.'

'I can't say I think that's really very wise,' he said, his black brows beetling. 'The people in the village are very old-fashioned, you know.'

'Maybe,' said Gabbie, annoyed that he should have jumped to conclusions again, and even more annoyed at his paternalistic attitude, 'but I'm not old-fashioned, and I shall have as many men to stay as I want!'

Michael opened his mouth about to reply, but then stopped, his lips tightening as he looked at Gabbie's defiant stare. Abruptly turning on his heel, he strode across to the kitchen door, where he turned and looked back at her. 'You are an impossible woman,' he said in a voice soft with controlled anger.

'I could say the same thing about you,' retorted Gabbie to his retreating back, 'only I'd change the gender!'

Whether or not he'd heard her she didn't know, as he didn't reply. The next thing she heard was the car door slam, and the engine start, then the swish of gravel as he spun the car round in the loose stones of the track that led to the cottage. She stood at the kitchen window, watching the headlamps of his car until they had disappeared in the direction of the twinkling lights of Aghios Nikolaos. For a long time she stood there in the silence which enveloped her, wishing with all her heart she hadn't been so proud and stubborn. She'd much rather have been down in the little town, with its myriad twinkling lights, than stuck up on a remote mountainside all alone; but she'd made her bed, so to speak, and now she had no alternative but to lie in it!

Much later, she reluctantly went to bed, taking a cup of wine up with her and the gas lantern. She tried to read, but the whole mountainside seemed to come alive in her imagination, every stunted bush seemed to have a life of its own, rustling as if inhabited by animals large and small. At last she began to feel sleepy, in spite of the rustlings, and was reassured when she'd put out the lantern and found the sky had cleared. The velvet blackness was pinpricked with millions of stars, the wind had died down and the air was warm and scented.

That thunderstorm really got under my skin, she thought sleepily, pulling up the covers tightly under her chin, it made me imagine all sorts of ridiculous things. Me, plain down-to-earth Gabrielle Kempson, who has always prided herself on being so sensible! Why, she almost laughed out loud, she had even imagined that Michael Nikolaides was nice and friendly—how ridiculous! But he *did* stay and keep you company, and he *did* help you get sorted out on your first evening, a voice at the back of her mind reminded her, and you *did* feel safe in his arms! Any port in a storm, she answered herself sleepily, before falling into a deep sleep from sheer exhaustion.

Next morning it was difficult to believe that the storm had ever happened. All traces of the pouring rain from the night before had disappeared and dried up in the first rays of the sun, and to her delight Gabbie found that the cottage was a positive sun-trap. She had a hasty breakfast from the remains of the loaf she had shared with Michael the night before, sitting on her little patio overlooking the now brilliant navy blue sea, that sparkled and reflected the clear jasmine light of morning. What she'd thought were ominous bushes, hiding creatures of the night, were in fact aromatic bushes of wild thyme and rosemary, interspersed with clumps of sweet-smelling sage and mint. Exotic-looking butterflies fluttered from bush to bush, spreading their wings to the warmth of the sun, and the busy bees were living up to their name, invisible to the eye, but the hum of their wings as they gathered in the nectar could be heard all around.

As she drove down to the clinic ready for the early morning start, she felt much happier. She hadn't made such a disastrous decision after all, it had just been unfortunate that her introduction to the cottage had coincided with a thunderstorm! And Michael Nikolaides hadn't exactly boosted her self-confidence much, with his disdainful suggestion that he didn't think she could cope.

Parking her car, she ran swiftly into the villa, knowing that Paulos would be awake and waiting to see her before she went on duty. Rounding the corner outside his room, she cannoned straight into Michael, obviously coming from visiting his father.

'Sleep well?' he asked, a Machiavellian look in his eyes.

'Like a log,' said Gabbie coolly, which was true; she omitted to mention that in fact it had taken her hours to get to sleep—that was an unimportant detail!

'Still intent on inviting your male friend?'

'Why should I change my mind?'

'Oh, I don't know, I just thought perhaps in the cold light of day . . .'

'I *never* change my mind,' snapped Gabbie, pushing past him as he made no effort to get out of the way. 'Now, if you'll excuse me.'

Once past him she scurried down the corridor, aware that Michael's dark eyes were following her every move, and was glad when she reached the peace and calm of Paulos' room. She could have easily have told him then that it was Peter her brother she intended to invite, but some obstinate devil inside her stopped the words. Let him think what he liked, she didn't care; but deep inside she knew, because of some totally illogical reason she couldn't fathom, she did care, and that very fact had made her rebel and behave in such a pigheaded manner.

'Everything all right?' Paulos asked her. His voice was weak, but three words strung together was the longest sentence Gabbie had heard him manage since his stroke.

'Everything is just fine,' she said gently, taking his hand and holding it between hers. 'I've moved into a little cottage just a few kilometres away, to take the load off Maria, and as soon as you're well, you're coming to dinner.'

A faint smile flickered across Paulos' face. 'Michael said,' he hesitated, searching for the words, 'very primitive,' he finally whispered.

'Don't you take any notice of whatever Michael has told you,' said Gabbie. 'He was very kind and helped me move in last night. He thinks it's a bit primitive, but I love it. It's a real change for me, being right in the countryside after living all the last few years cooped up in the grime of London!'

Paulos laughed, and Gabbie knew that Michael had given his father a blow-by-blow account of the cottage on the hillside, had probably even told him that she hadn't known how to light the gas lantern or stove.

'I'll come in again later today,' said Gabbie, glancing at her watch. 'I mustn't be late, your son is a real slavedriver, you know!' Although she smiled and said the words lightly as she bent over to kiss Paulos' pale face, it was the truth. And of one thing she was absolutely determined, she would not give the new Medical Director any cause to criticise her work. By the time she'd finished at the Kriti Institute she'd have him eating his words, he'd have to tell her that she had been the right appointment! Quite how she was going achieve that miracle she wasn't sure, nevertheless that was her aim.

It was Friday, and Friday afternoons Gabbie

gave seminars for the more experienced nurses. On arrival at her office she found Michael standing by her desk, her schedule of teaching sessions in his hand.

'Endo-tracheal intubation for group three, I see for today,' he said, looking up as she came in.

'Yes,' said Gabbie.

'Sam tells me these seminars have been going very well.'

'I think so.' Gabbie wondered what was coming next.

'So long as you don't let any of them think they can run before they can walk,' he said, replacing the papers on her desk.

'Dr Nikolaides, I do know what I'm doing, and you'll have to trust me.' Any friendliness she had felt towards him the previous night evaporated at the implication of his words.

'As I said at the interview, if I remember correctly,' he replied smoothly, 'only time will tell.'

'It will indeed, Dr Nikolaides,' said Gabbie as calmly as possible, pushing her hands deep into the pockets of her white uniform, the temptation to reach up and slap that proud, hawklike face towering above her proving almost irresistible! The colour of her eyes changed from sapphire to a steely blue, as silently she challenged him to say something else derogatory.

But he said nothing, merely gave a faint smile, shrugged his muscular shoulders and left, walking down the corridor towards Theatres where Gabbie knew he had a morning's operating ahead of him.

CHAPTER FIVE

IT WAS Friday the thirteenth of June—not that Gabbie was in the least superstitious, but as the day wore on she did begin to wonder if there was something in the old wives' tale of everything going wrong on Friday the thirteenth. She had planned a quiet morning of preparing notes on intravenous infusion, and had just typed out a list of terminology; that had put her behind schedule for a start, as her typing was painfully slow, but Valissa had a mountain of work dictated by Michael and Sam, and couldn't possibly do it for her. Now, however, she had finished the stencil and was reading through it proudly, not too many white blobs where she'd had to correct.

'Infiltration: deposit or diffusion of substances not normal to it. Parenteral: not through the alimentary canal (e.g. by subcutaneous or intravenous injection.) Phlebitis: inflammation . . .' Her checking out loud came to an abrupt halt as Sophie burst through the door without stopping to knock first. Her normally cheerful sunny face was worried and frightened.

'Can you come quick to emergency admissions? Sam needs help and I think you are the best one to help.'

In a split second Gabbie was running down the

corridor towards the tiny emergency admission area, Sophie at her side. 'What's the emergency?' she asked.

'Baby needs resuscitation, fallen in the swimming pool.' Sophie was beginning to pant, this was her second lap of the long corridor.

Gabbie didn't need to ask further questions. As they arrived she saw Sam struggling alone with a small child about eighteen months old.

'Take care not to hyperextend the neck,' muttered Sam as together they manoeuvred the child into the position for checking the airway and cardiac massage.

Gabbie nodded, then while Sam positioned himself over the mouth and nose of the infant and started mouth-to-mouth, one breath for every five cardiac compressions, Gabbie did the cardiac compressions. They hadn't even spoken to each other about the method to be used, both knew that on such a small infant this was the best way; the nurse's hands being more delicate for the compression of an infant's chest, and the doctor able to pump more air through the oral airways. They worked solidly for about two minutes, Gabbie using her fingertips in the mid-sternum, knowing the ventricles of a child's heart were anatomically higher than those of an adult because of the size of the child's liver.

She looked at Sam. Beads of perspiration were standing out on his forehead, and she was vaguely aware of Sophie trying to keep the frantic parents back out of the way. She could feel the perspiration beginning to break out on her own brow; time was running out, and still there was no response. She wondered whether any minute Sam would resort to mechanical defibrillation.

'Get the defibrillator ready at the side,' she said to Sophie, but even as she spoke she saw the expression change on Sam's face.

He had been feeling the femoral pulse while she had been doing cardiac compression. 'We've won!' he said, letting his breath out in a long-drawn-out sigh of relief. 'We'll give him a burst of high-concentration oxygen on the face mask, then I'll intubate and we'll keep him on the blower for a few hours.'

Gabbie held the oxygen mask on, while Sam got the right sized laryngoscope ready. As soon as everything was prepared by Sam and Sophie, Gabbie removed the mask and switched off the oxygen; then gently she flexed the baby's head while Sam introduced the laryngoscope blade into his mouth. Then under direct visition he expertly slid in the lubricated Magill paediatric endo-tracheal tube, and proceeded to connect the child to the ventilator. Only then did he turn to the child's parents, who had been hovering in the back-ground all this time.

'We'll keep Janni on this respirator for a while, just to be on the safe side, and now I'm going to check his reflexes.'

'Will he be all right?' The mother, a tiny little woman, approached timidly, looking anxiously at her baby connected up to the ventilator.

Gabbie felt a rush of pity for her. The little boy looked so lost, lying with tubing from his mouth connected to the machine at his side, the bellows clicking gently as they inflated and deflated his lungs. For her the sight held no terrors, but on top of the trauma they must have suffered at finding their child unconscious in the swimming pool, seeing his tiny form connected up to a clicking mass of machinery, she knew, must be horrifying.

'We can't say for certain,' said Sam briefly, looking harassed.

'Sophie, you take Mr and Mrs Thakis to the *kafénion* and get them some coffee, while Sam and I do the tests,' said Gabbie, knowing Sam wanted them out of the way.

Sophie nodded and said something in rapid Greek to the couple, Gabbie smiled at them encouragingly, and escorted them firmly to the door. 'We'll see you in a little while,' she said, and Sophie translated.

Instinctively she knew Sam feared the worst, that the child had been unconscious too long and that irreversible brain damage had occurred. As if echoing her thoughts Sam said, 'I think we wasted our time.' He looked tired and defeated.

'Let's find out first, not jump to conclusions,' said Gabbie firmly. But although she put a determinedly brave face on, in her heart of hearts she thought Sam was probably right.

An hour later, however, she and Sam were smiling at each other across the ventilator. The chest X-ray had been normal, the blood gases well on the way to normality and little Janni responded positively to stimulation, and had at that very moment opened his eyes on command. He was going to make a full recovery.

'Thank you, Sister, for keeping me going,' said Sam, reaching across and grabbing her hand. 'I *do* believe in miracles now!'

'So do I,' said Gabbie, feeling an irrational hot prick of tears behind her eyelids, 'and on Friday the thirteenth too!'

'I'll go and speak to the parents,' said Sam. 'You stay here.'

'And get a coffee while you're there,' said Gabbie gently. 'You look as if you could do with a little resuscitation yourself!'

It was nearly lunchtime before she eventually got back to her office, having settled little Janni in a side room, his now happy parents sitting by his side. A junior nurse was in attendance, having been given strict instructions by Gabbie on what to monitor, and to send for Sam or herself if anything should change; but she was happy in her own mind that from now on all would be well.

What was left of the morning passed by in a flash as she finished preparing her lecture, only snatching a quick coffee and a pastry in the *kafénion*; there was no time for a leisurely lunch, she had to do some shopping if she was to eat that night. So, still munching on the pastry, she dashed down into the town, parking her car in the little square, from where she could get with ease to all the shops she needed. Hurrying from the butchers to the bakers, where the smell of hot bread reminded her she was still hungry on to the little general stores where everything was piled high in haphazard heaps, she got everything on her list, and staggered back to the car, plastic bags bursting at the seams.

Glancing at her watch, she saw she still had a little time left, time enough for a cool drink at one of the tavernas that fringed the square. Choosing a seat in the shade of a fragrant citrus tree, she ordered a Coke and leaned back. It was relaxing in the cool of the shade watching the old men at the next table, worry beads clicking through their fingers as they sipped their tiny strong black coffees, washed down with the inevitable glasses of water.

She watched the townspeople coming and going; they were easily distinguishable from the tourists, who all wore shorts and sundresses. The majority of Greeks, especially the older ones, dressed in black and other dark colours as if it was winter. As Gabbie watched, she realised that although she had been on the island nearly a month, she had in fact seen very little. Still, tomorrow is the weekend, she consoled herself. She had to work on Saturday morning, but after that the time was her own. She would explore a little then, but suddenly she remembered Sam had offered to take her snorkelling on Saturday afternoon—she'd almost forgotten.

Much as she would have liked to have stayed there, she had no more time to linger, and quickly finishing the ice-cool Coke, she left and made her way back to the Institute. Before making her way to the seminar room, she dumped her shopping in the relative cool of the Institute's kitchen.

She had set out all the papers needed and drawn a diagram on the blackboard, and was sitting awaiting the arrival of her group when Sam appeared. 'I'm afraid I'm going to interrupt you again,' he said.

'What now?' asked Gabbie, wondering what else had gone wrong.

'Well, Michael is still in the operating theatre, there was an additional case to the list, and I gather all is not going smoothly. So that means he can't go out to the Alexiou house at Sitea, so I must go instead.'

'And?' Gabbie raised her eyebrows. 'Where do I fit into all this?'

'Sotiris Alexiou has asthma, and is having a bad attack—his parents have just phoned, he needs an injection of noradrenaline by the sound of it, so I must go and not waste time. But a child has just come in with acute dehydration after a bout of diarrhoea, and needs intravenous infusion. If I set up the régime and prepare the solution, will you administer it? I know you can do it, you're the only nurse here who could.'

Gabbie stood up. 'Of course I will, let's not waste time. I can teach while I'm doing it, it will do the girls good to see the technique in actual practice.'

Sam smiled. 'You think of everything,' he said, hurrying back down the corridor.

He was as good as his word and prepared the prescribed solution, then left hurriedly, his mind obviously on the Alexiou child out at Sitea. It was another town on the coast some kilometres away, and Gabbie didn't bother him with unnecessary questions; he had to get there quickly; asthma attacks were real life-threateners sometimes if help didn't arrive in time, so she appreciated his need for haste.

The four nurses who formed the advanced group stood at Gabbie's request, well back from the child she was about to prepare for intravenous infusion. 'In this case,' she explained, 'it's being performed to provide basic nutrition and hydration.'

Carefully she shaved part of the infant's head, explaining as she went along that the largest and most easily accessible vein in the child was located in the temporal skull region. 'There is also less likelihood that the needle will become dislodged after insertion if this area is used,' she told them.

Asking Sophie first to cleanse the skin surface and then to hold the infant's head, she carefully slid the needle into the tiny vein. This was always a tricky thing to do, especially in a small child, and Gabbie breathed a silent sigh of relief when she saw that the needle had entered the vein cleanly.

The intravenous solution Sam had prepared was placed on the special stand that held the giving set, and Gabbie explained that it was essential that it should be approximately forty-five to sixty centimetres above the level of the vein, so that gravity would be sufficient to overcome venous pressure.

'As you see,' she said, indicating that the nurses should come a little closer, 'the weight of the tubing could pull the needle out of the vein, so it must be anchored to prevent tension on the needle entry site. This can be done with tape, but making sure enough slack is left to allow easy manoeuvrability.'

She beckoned Eleni to come over. 'Would you like to secure the tubing?'

Eleni nodded nervously. 'Yes,' she said, her hands trembling a little as she carefully followed Gabbie's instructions.

'Now,' said Gabbie, 'we must regulate the flow, it is very important to do this, and the doctor will always tell you how he wants it. Infants cannot tolerate too much intravenous fluid too quickly, and the rate must run at the exact rate prescribed by the paediatrician, in this case Dr Jones. Now, can any of you tell me why I should say it is important that the rate should be adjusted while the infant is quiet? Which,' she added with a smile, 'luckily for us, this particular one is!'

There was silence for a moment, then Sophie said, 'Is it because the blood vessels constrict when a child is crying, and you'd get a false reading?'

Gabbie smiled; they were learning well. 'Good,' she said. 'Yes, that's it precisely. Dr Jones had prescribed twenty-four millilitres per hour and this intravenous set yields ten drops per millilitre, thus the rate of flow equals ten times twenty-four divided by sixty, which is four drops per minute.' As she was speaking she pre-set the infusion pump.

Asking Eleni and Olga to help her, she showed them how to wedge the infant firmly in with restrainers on either side to prevent too much movement, then she gave Sophie the task of staying with the baby.

'The fluid rate must be checked every hour,' said Gabbie, handing her the record chart, 'and an accurate intake and output record is absolutely essential.'

Sophie bobbed her head as she listened, pleased that she had been the one put in charge. 'And I can call you if I'm worried about anything?' she asked.

'Of course you must. Don't wait a moment. I shall be in my office until Dr Jones returns.' Gabbie turned and was about to dismiss the other girls back to their posts for the rest of the afternoon, when she was suddenly aware of the tall frame of Michael Nikolaides filling the doorway. 'How long have . . . ?' she began.

'Long enough,' he said grimly, nodding abruptly at the girls, who without a word got the message and left the room. He didn't have to tell them to leave, one look at his thunderous black face was enough.

Without a word he strode across to the now peacefully sleeping baby, inspected the entry site of the needle, checked the drip rate of the intravenous set, then looked at Sophie. 'Call *me* if anything goes wrong,' he grated. 'There's no need to bother Sister Kempson.'

A hot flush of anger flared in Gabbie's stomach. The tone of his voice seemed to indicate that he didn't think she'd be much use if anything did go wrong. The fact that she'd set up a perfect intravenous drip seemed to have escaped his notice completely. 'I . . .' she began.

'I'll talk to you in the privacy of your office,' he said, gripping her elbow and propelling her along the corridor at breakneck speed.

Gabbie opened her mouth to protest, then thought better of it. He was obviously bent on a confrontation over some matter; better to have it out in the privacy of her office as he had suggested. She had noticed Sophie's inquisitive black eyes darting from one to the other, taking everything in. Anything she overheard would be all over the Institute in a matter of hours, Gabbie knew that, and even more so if it concerned the new English nurse, as she was called by practically everyone.

The novelty of her arrival hadn't worn off, and slightly to Gabbie's mild annoyance her movements and pronouncements on every topic were passed from person to person with the speed of the jungle telegraph. So she kept her mouth shut, drawn into a straight line of annoyance and vainly tried to wrench her elbow from the vicelike grip of the hand grasping it.

Once inside her office, however, he let her go, having first swung her round to face him, then leaning against the door to survey her from his towering height.

Again that feeling of being swamped by something entirely out of her control swept over her, but she fought against it and stood her ground. 'What do you mean by dragging me away from the patient in that manner and pushing me in here?' she stormed.

'I thought we came in here for privacy,' said Michael, his voice irritatingly smooth. 'If you shout like that the whole of Aghios Nikolaos will have an early awakening from its siesta.'

'I haven't had a siesta!' shouted Gabbie. 'I've been working like a slave all day, and . . .' Suddenly the truth of his words struck home and she hastily lowered her voice. 'And I've just performed quite a difficult procedure, so I'm not in the mood for any of your histrionics.'

It was not the way to speak to the Medical Director of the Institute, but something about Michael Nikolaides made her lose her cool; he can sack me if he wants, she thought mutinously.

'That's the whole point,' Michael's voice was icily controlled. '*You* did the procedure, which you know very well should have been done by a doctor. I don't have many rules in my handbook, but the initiation of intravenous therapy is one of them.'

'There wasn't a doctor available, and Sam—I mean Dr Jones—thought I was perfectly capable. He prescribed the solution and the flow rate, I merely set it up. And I dare you,' she added, almost standing on tiptoe so that she could glare more effectively into his unreadable, inky black eyes, 'I dare you to find fault with what I've done.'

'Where is Sam?'

'He's gone to a place called Sitea, apparently a child called . . .' Gabbie hesitated, trying to remember the name.

'Sotiris Alexiou?'

'Yes, that's it, had a severe asthma attack. Sam

thought he needed an injection. At the same time another baby came in dehydrated, neither case could wait, and you were still in the middle of operating.'

'I see,' said Michael slowly. 'That explains it.'

'I could have explained it just as well back there, without you flying off the handle, and dragging me in here. Whatever must the other nurses think!'

'Perhaps they thought I brought you in here to ravish you,' said Michael, suddenly grinning.

'It's not funny! I'm deadly serious, I won't be treated like that!' Gabbie snapped.

'All right, I apologise for not asking you properly, and wrongly jumping to conclusions. I thought you'd overstepped yourself in your desire to show the other girls how good you were.'

'You *always* think the wrong thing, I don't know why I bother to stay here,' flared Gabbie. 'You obviously have no faith in me whatsoever!'

'It's not that so much, but I worry that the other girls will be tempted to try something they're not capable of. I had my doubts about that subject on your list, intravenous therapy, but actually demonstrating it to them is . . .'

'The best way of teaching,' said Gabbie angrily. 'Give me, and your nurses, some credit for common sense. Of course they know they can't perform it, but they needed to feel included, not excluded, from difficult techniques. Nurses can and do things that doctors can do, and sometimes, as today, there's no alternative. One day, one of these girls might be on her own in some other place, where the skills she has learnt will be needed.'

'My, my!' Michael leaned further back against the door, looking down at her, amusement plainly flickering in his eyes. 'You do get all het up, don't you, Miss Kempson!'

'Yes, I do,' said Gabbie coldly, 'especially when there are some doctors about like you, who think they're God, and that nurses are merely menial subjects, put on this earth for the sole purpose of fetching and carrying at their command!'

'Aren't they?' he said. 'I thought they were.'

'Well, that's where you're wrong!' hissed Gabbie, now almost beside herself with rage. 'One day the twentieth century will even reach Crete and the women here, then look out!'

'I have a nasty feeling it already has,' observed Michael dryly. Then he added with a laugh, 'But instead of arriving sedately on the back of Old Father Time, it came in the suitcase of a certain Miss Kempson!'

Gabbie rewarded him with another glare, and sat herself behind her desk. 'If you've nothing more to say, I've paperwork to catch up on,' she said stiffly.

'Yes.' Michael came towards the desk, and placing one of his hands on the corner leaned over her, with the other hand he traced the outline of her face. Against her better instincts Gabbie stared at him, mesmerised by the dancing lights in his eyes, frissons of electricity running the length of her spine.

'You are like Pandora,' he said softly, 'you brought your box and you opened it. Only yours was full of all the silly feminist notions of the twentieth century.'

'Well, if the legend is to be believed,' said Gabbie sweetly, recovering her equilibrium as he removed his hand, 'the only thing left in the box was Hope, which lay at the bottom. So I suppose I can always *hope* you'll change your chauvinistic views!'

'I shouldn't count on it,' said Michael with a mischievous smile as he stood up, then walked across to the door. 'I believe there is a distinct place on earth for men and women, and it's clearly defined that man shall be the master.'

'Oh . . . !' Gabbie picked up the nearest book and threw it, missing him as he closed the door smartly behind him; the book fell with a dull thud to the floor. Gabbie stared at the book, wishing she'd thrown it harder and sooner. That man was testing her patience to the very limit! Then the thought occurred to her, perhaps he really did want to drive her away, and was trying to manoeuvre her into handing in her notice. Well, if that's your little game, she thought defiantly, it won't work. She had promised Paulos she would stay, and stay she would, no matter how objectionable his son might be!

CHAPTER SIX

THAT EVENING Gabbie unloaded her shopping, which she had forgotten and left behind in the Institute's kitchen, having to turn round and go back for it, a fact which did nothing to improve her already soured temper. Having put everything away, she poured herself a glass of wine, feeling she deserved it after her traumatic afternoon, and dragged a chair from the kitchen out on to the patio.

It was a gorgeous evening, warm and still, the sun slowly sinking down behind the sea, a great crimson orb, splashing everything in sight a delicate pink. Pink sky at night, shepherd's delight, thought Gabbie, at last beginning to relax; it was impossible not to with such a magnificent panorama spread out before her.

A small tortoiseshell-coloured cat appeared from nowhere, and wrapped itself affectionately around her legs. 'How did you get here?' said Gabbie, stroking its thin back. 'Where do you live?' The cat sat down, leaning companionably against her legs.

But it finally began to get dark, and she went indoors to light the lamp. It followed her in, mewing piteously when she cut some bread. A piece of crust dropped to the floor, to be pounced on by the cat and devoured ravenously. 'Poor little thing,' said Gabbie softly, 'you must be starving!'

She had a tin of pilchards in the cupboard, and opening it, she mashed some of the pilchards with some bread and put a saucerful down. It vanished in a trice, then a saucer of milk disappeared the same way. After that the cat inspected the cottage from top to bottom, finally decided Gabbie's bed was the best place to sleep, curling herself into a ball and purring loudly. Gabbie knew then she had a permanent lodger, but she didn't mind, it was company and the cat didn't seem to belong to anyone, so she named her Aphrodite and politely moved her from the bed, making up a chair with an old blanket.

'That's your bed,' she told Aphrodite, who looked at her with enormous yellow eyes and purred loudly at her good fortune.

Next morning dawned bright and beautiful, the sea a translucent aquamarine; Gabbie marvelled at the view, for ever changing before her eyes, a kaleidoscope of colours, never the same. She was growing to like the cottage more and more in spite of its lack of amenities. She had even got used to the primitive loo, and the lack of a bathroom and shower didn't bother her; she could always use those at the Institute. As it was Saturday, she only had the morning duty to do, and was planning to catch up on her teaching schedule. The programme was already worked out, but the finite details and the general information sheets had to be typed; she didn't want to overload Valissa, the very willing secretary, at the last minute. All was quiet at the Institute when she arrived, having first slipped in to visit Paulos and Maria as she always did.

'I worry about you, all alone up there on the mountain.' Maria's motherly face was concerned. Now that Paulos was obviously on the road to recovery, she had resumed her interest in everything around her; at first her only concern had been for her husband.

'I'm perfectly all right,' Gabbie reassured her, 'and I've even acquired a cat now, a dear little tortoiseshell female.'

Paulos had overheard them talking as they walked down towards his room. 'A cat,' he said, smiling. His smile was still lopsided from the partial paralysis of his right side, but his speech was improving daily. 'That means you really do intend to stay.'

'I've always told you I would,' said Gabbie, 'and I meant it.'

'Yes, I know,' said Paulos, 'but Michael says . . .'

'Don't take any notice of whatever Michael says,' interrupted Gabbie firmly, half of her dying to know just what it was that Michael had said, the other half stubbornly refusing to let Paulos finish his sentence.

'I hope Michael is behaving himself,' murmured his mother, looking at Gabbie reflectively.

Gabbie pulled a face. 'It depends what you mean by behaving,' she said. 'We do have our professional disagreements,' she admitted; there was no point in not admitting it. After all, Michael had probably confided in his father that he thought she had overstepped the mark with the intravenous infusion. 'However,' she added, 'I think I can deal with those.'

'Oh,' said Maria, suddenly all smiles, 'only professional disagreements.'

'Why, yes.' Gabbie was surprised at Maria's sudden beaming smile. 'What other sort should we have?'

'I'll get you a coffee before you go on duty.' Maria bustled busily from the room, still smiling.

Paulos beckoned Gabbie nearer. 'You'll have to forgive Maria,' he said slowly, but he was smiling his lopsided smile. 'She's an inveterate match-maker—any unmarried female is sized up as a potential wife for Michael!'

'I somehow have the feeling that if your son ever marries, *he* will make the decision,' remarked Gabbie dryly, 'and it certainly won't be to an emancipated Englishwoman!'

Maria came hurrying back with a tray set with three coffee cups, and Paulos didn't pursue the topic of conversation. 'You must come to lunch tomorrow,' she said, passing the coffee across to Gabbie, before propping up her husband so that he could manage to drink his unaided. 'We'll have a leisurely lunch, and then you can swim in the afternoon if you wish. Michael is on duty, unfortunately, so he probably won't be here, but never mind.'

Gabbie accepted gratefully. It would be nice to

have a family meal with Maria and Paulos, and the fact that Michael would be absent made the prospect even more pleasant. She'd be really able to relax, no tension, wondering what comment was coming next!

The coffee finished, she made her way across to the Institute, pausing for a moment to drink in the beauty of the vivid purple bougainvillea that splashed its way across the side of the building. Each petal caught the rays of the sun, and reflected back its own little individual spot of light; the combination of the long white building, the incandescent purple and the clear azure sky was breathtaking, and Gabbie drank in the scene gratefully.

She had had a letter from Peter only the day before, and he had told her it had rained almost continually since she had left England. It's very depressing, he had said in his letter, grey day following grey day. She could well imagine it, but here in Crete in the clear bright light, the sun greeting her every time she opened her eyes, it was difficult to imagine feeling depressed; she was sure it accounted for the sunny disposition of almost everyone she had met so far. The exception being the Medical Director, Michael Nikolaides; he seemed to carry his own personal thundercloud around with him, she reflected wryly.

The Institute was busy with the early morning activities. Sam had gone out to Sitea to visit the Alexiou child again, and Michael, for once smiling

one of his dazzling smiles, had stuck his head into
her office to tell her he was going down in the town
for a short while, so she was in charge.

'Are you sure you can trust me?' Gabbie couldn't
refrain from asking, remembering their altercation
of the previous afternoon.

'Of course,' he had said. 'Nothing will happen,
and anyway, I know you're very capable.'

Gabbie shook her head in exasperation when he
had left. He seemed to have a very short memory!
But she felt pleased nevertheless, and plodded on
steadily with her paperwork until she was interrupted by a frantic-looking Eleni.

What now? thought Gabbie with a sigh of resignation as she saw Eleni's worried face. 'It's the
Mayor's son, two-year-old Andreas—he's swallowed a whole bottle of aspirin. The Mayor, Mr
Lukas Bokas, is very angry because Dr Nikolaides
is not here.' She gasped the words out and looked
very frightened, and when Gabbie came face to
face with Mr Bokas, a huge fat bully of a man, she
could see why.

He seemed less concerned that his son might die
if not treated promptly than with the fact that he
had not been greeted with the proper formalities by
the Director of the hospital, which he felt he should
have as befitted his station in life, namely that of
Mayor.

'I demand to see Dr Nikolaides,' he said to
Gabbie, bringing down his clenched fist aggress-
ively on the small table in the emergency reception
area. He shouted the words in Greek at Eleni, who

Capture all the excitement, intrigue and emotion of the busy world of medicine
Take 4 free Doctor/Nurse Romances as your introductory gift from Mills & Boon.

The fascinating real-life drama of modern medical life provides the thrilling background to these gripping stories of desire, heartbreak, passion and true love. And to introduce you to this marvellous series, we'll send you 4 Doctor Nurse titles and an exclusive Mills & Boon Tote Bag, absolutely FREE when you complete and return this card.

We'll also reserve a subscription for you to the Mills & Boon Reader Service, which means you'll enjoy:

☆ SIX WONDERFUL NOVELS — sent direct to you every two months.
☆ FREE POSTAGE & PACKING — we pay all the extras.
☆ FREE REGULAR NEWSLETTER — packed with competitions, author news and much more. . . .
☆ SPECIAL OFFERS — selected exclusively for our subscribers.

There's no obligation or commitment — you can cancel your subscription at any time. Simply complete and return this card today to receive your free introductory gifts. No stamp is required.

Free Books Certificate

Dear Susan,

Please send me my 4 free Doctor Nurse Romances together with my Mills & Boon tote bag. Please also reserve a special Reader Service subscription for me. If I decide to subscribe, I shall, from the beginning of the month following my free parcel of books, receive 6 superb new titles every two months for just £7.20, post and packing free. If I decide not to subscribe, I shall write to you within 10 days. The free books and Tote Bag will be mine to keep in any case.

I understand that I am under no obligation whatsoever — I can cancel my subscription at any time simply by writing to you. I am over 18 years of age.

Your exclusive FREE
Mills & Boon Tote Bag

Name: _____
(BLOCK CAPITALS PLEASE)

Address: _____

_____ Signature _____

_____ Postode _____

1A8D

To Susan Welland
Mills & Boon Reader Service
FREEPOST
Croydon
Surrey
CR9 9EL

SEND NO MONEY NOW

translated rapidly, shooting anxious glances at
Gabbie.

'Dr Nikolaides will be back in a few moments,'
lied Gabbie, frantically praying that he would. 'In
the meantime I'll begin treatment on your son.'
While Eleni translated, Gabbie pushed Mr Bokas
aside and bent to examine the child, vaguely noticing the downtrodden little woman hovering
anxiously behind the bulk of Mr Bokas. The boy
was already hyperventilating, and putting her hand
on his brow, she felt the fever without needing to
take his temperature.

'How many aspirins did he swallow?' she asked
quickly.

Mr Bokas shrugged when Eleni translated. 'Who
can say?' was his reply. 'Where is Dr Nikolaides?'

'How many?' persisted Gabbie, and looked at
Eleni. 'Tell them it is very important that I should
have some idea.'

At this the woman answered timidly, venturing
out from behind the Mayor, 'It was a full bottle, a
hundred perhaps.'

'Thank you.' Gabbie gave a reassuring smile in
the anxious woman's direction. 'Eleni, would you
tell them I'm going to do an immediate gastric
lavage, and ask Mr and Mrs Bokas to wait outside.'
She indicated the waiting area outside the
emergency room.

Mr Bokas planted his large feet firmly apart and
announced that as he was the Mayor he was going
to stay.

Gabbie lost her temper. 'I don't care who you

are,' she said, nodding to a startled Eleni to trans-
late, 'but we can't work on your son without adequ-
ate space.' Before the angry Mayor could say
another word, she grasped his fat arm and pro-
pelled him without further ado into the corridor
outside. 'Wait here,' she snapped the words out
like staccato machine-gun bullets, 'until I call you.'
So ferocious was her expression that even Mr
Bokas was taken aback and needed no translation.
With his timid wife at his side, he obediently did as
he was told.

Without giving him or what she'd done another
thought, Gabbie returned to the child lying on the
emergency couch. They had already wasted valu-
able time, and she wasted no more, immediately
embarking on the gastric lavage through a naso-
gastric tube. She worked quickly and efficiently,
snapping out commands to Eleni, who assisted her,
and between them they retrieved a large number of
tablets from the child's stomach still intact, but not
a hundred.

'He'll have to stay in,' said Gabbie to Eleni.
'Arrange a bed for him, while I take some blood
samples.' As she spoke she was already taking the
sample and capping the specimen bottle.

'Blood samples?' queried Eleni, looking even
more worried.

'Yes, we'll have to check his blood gases, electro-
lytes, blood count, clotting ability and liver func-
tion. If he really took a hundred aspirins I'm afraid
he may well suffer some renal and liver damage.'
Gabbie glanced at her watch; it had only been

fifteen minutes, but it had felt like ten hours. 'Oh, where is Dr Nikolaides?' she sighed, voicing the thoughts of both of them, Eleni and herself.

As if in answer to her question the door opened and Michael strode in. He listened as Gabbie told him what she had done and nodded. 'Good,' he looked towards Eleni. 'You get the bed organised as Sister Kempson asked, and I will accompany young Andreas to the ward while Sister takes that blood up to the lab. And tell the technician it has priority over everything else,' he added. 'He shouldn't be too busy this morning.'

Gabbie looked at the child stirring on the couch. His colour was good; perhaps they had been in time after all. 'What do you think?' she asked.

But before Michael could answer, the door burst open and the ebullient form of Mr Bokas loomed in the doorway. He spoke to Michael in rapid Greek, but Gabbie understood enough to know he was asking about his son Andreas. 'We'll be keeping him in for observation,' replied Michael in English. Gabbie was surprised and felt annoyed—Mr Bokas had let her think he couldn't speak English.

The Mayor, for his part, glowered at Gabbie and pointed an accusing finger. 'That woman, she has no respect, she drives me from this room. She must go—Greek nurses are better!'

Gabbie opened her mouth about to reply, but was silenced by Michael with an abrupt wave of his hand. 'You go with Andreas to the ward, get someone else to deliver the blood sample, and I will talk to Mr Bokas.' Then with a quiet smile, he indicated that the Mayor should accompany him, and Gabbie watched them walk together towards Michael's office, Mrs Bokas trailing along behind.

There was nothing she could do, but inwardly she seethed. There was no necessity for Michael to apologise on her behalf—the wretched man might be the Mayor, but he had been a nuisance nonetheless. However, she put her ruffled feelings aside, found someone to take the blood to the lab, and concentrated on settling a by now livelier by the minute Andreas into the ward.

'I think you'll have your hands full,' she said to the nurse in charge as she departed. 'I was worried that some permanent damage might have been done, but judging by his rapid recovery I think not.'

The nurse smiled, and gave Andreas a wooden train, which he proceeded to dismantle in a vigorous fashion, while Gabbie left, glad that she didn't have the rumbustious youngster in her charge for the rest of the day!

She finished the work in her office, finally catching up on the paperwork at last, without seeing anything more of either Michael or Mr Bokas. As she drove her little Fiat back towards the cottage, she thought about the scene in the emergency room, and then about the way Michael had taken Mr Bokas off to his office, and her feeling of anger returned. The very least Michael could have done was to have supported her—after all, she had saved Andreas' life, but no, what did he do? At this very moment he was probably still entertaining fat Mr Bokas to coffee. She could just imagine him agreeing that English nurses were impossible, that they didn't know their place in society! After all, that had been the gist of what he'd said to her the previous afternoon.

On arrival at her cottage she was greeted enthusiastically by Aphrodite, who had been sleeping in the sun on the patio. 'At least you're glad to see me,' said Gabbie, stroking her shiny fur, as the little cat wound herself like a snake around her bare legs. Although she was a small cat, her purr more than compensated for her lack of size, it was so loud she sounded like a small outboard motor.

After feeding Aphrodite again, who seemed permanently hungry, Gabbie made herself a salad and set up the kitchen table outside in the shade of the small olive tree that clung to the side of the cottage; then putting on her bikini she ate, then lay out on the sun-lounger she had borrowed, at Maria's insistence, from the villa. The food made her feel sleepy, and she dozed in the sun, listening to the contented rumble of Aphrodite, who had taken up position under the sunbed in the shade. The hillside shimmered in the heat of early afternoon. I ought to go in, she thought sleepily, I'll get burned; that was her last conscious thought before being awakened by the feel of a finger being slowly drawn down her body, from the base of her throat to her navel.

'Don't you know it's dangerous to sleep in the afternoon sun?' Michael's voice was disapproving.

With a start, Gabbie sat bolt upright, blinking against the glare of the sunlight. 'What are you doing here?' she demanded.

'Saving you from a severe case of sunburn, by the look of it,' replied Michael, his eyes lingering appreciatively on the fluid lines of her body, exposed to advantage by the tiny blue bikini which perfectly matched the colour of her eyes.

Gabbie pushed back her hair, bleached even blonder by the strong Cretan sun, and regarded him suspiciously, then immediately wished she'd left it hanging in a curtain across her face. That way he wouldn't have been able to see the faint flush she was unable to control. It was the way he was looking at her—he might have said she was flat-chested like a boy, but his expression at that moment indicated that perhaps he might have revised his opinion. Gabbie knew the bikini displayed her slim figure to advantage, and had been pleased with it when she had bought in a Covent Garden boutique; although now, irrationally, she was wishing she was wearing a plain black one-piece!

'I never burn,' she said, but got up nevertheless, and moved into the shade. 'And that can't be the reason you came,' she added, picking up the towel lying on the back of the chair and draping it around her shoulders. Covered up a little, she felt more composed, able to look him straight in the eye.

'I came to talk to you about Mr Bokas,' said Michael.

'There's nothing I want to talk about, only Andreas. Is he still making a good recovery?'

'Yes, he is, but Mr Bokas said . . .'

'Nothing that Mr Bokas said, or for that matter what you have got to say, is of the slightest interest to me,' said Gabbie icily, remembering the way Michael had stopped her from justifying herself back at the Institute; just accepting the wretched Mayor's word for it that she had no respect, and should be dismissed!

Aphrodite caused a sudden diversion. Suddenly aware that Gabbie's comforting presence was no longer on the lounger, she dived out from beneath it, and immediately transferred her affections to Michael. Almost standing on her nose, and making a noise like a liner at full throttle in an effort to gain his attention. Fickle female! thought Gabbie, watching her squirm around his legs.

He bent down and picked her up. 'New room-mate?' he said, raising his dark brows quizzically.

'That's Aphrodite—I've adopted her,' said Gabbie, watching the small cat wriggling ecstatically in his hands. Fascinated, she watched as he held her. How large his hands were, but how long and sensitively tapered were his fingers. After a moment he returned her to the patio.

'Your family will soon be increasing,' he said briefly, 'any day now.'

Gabbie frowned. 'What do you mean . . . ?' she began in a puzzled voice.

Michael threw his head back and roared with laughter. 'You've named her rightly, the goddess of love. She has already been loved, and is pregnant!'

'Oh dear!' Gabbie watched Aphrodite as she made her way in through the kitchen door, then progressed very purposefully up towards the bed-room.

'You can always drown them,' said Michael.

'Oh no, I couldn't possibly! How dare you suggest such a thing!'

'Just trying to be helpful,' said Michael with an irritating grin, picking up a fresh fig from the table and biting into it.

'I don't call that being helpful, I call that being cruel,' said Gabbie. 'I'll keep her and her kittens.'

'So there *is* a chink in your armour after all,' observed Michael, throwing the fig stalk down the mountainside. 'You're not as tough as you think you are—and now, to get back to the business of Mr Bokas.'

'I told you a moment ago I have absolutely no intention of talking about it,' said Gabbie, 'and now, if you'll excuse me . . .' She started to pass him, intending to enter the kitchen, but one hand snaked out, catching her wrist, and he swung her round so that she faced him. 'I meant it!' she gasped, trying to wriggle her hand free, but some-how the other became imprisoned too.

Slowly, without any hurry, Michael drew her towards him. His mouth curved in a sensual smile. Gabbie's heart started behaving in the most alarm-ing fashion, thumping so loudly against her rib cage that the beat of it rang in her ears.

'Perhaps you're not the ice maiden you appear to be,' he said softly, just before he lowered his lips to hers.

For a moment she resisted, holding her body

tense and rigid, but then the demanding mastery of his kiss triumphed, and she relaxed against him, lifting her face willingly to his, parting her lips for his exploring tongue. She felt drugged, eager to give herself, as his hands moved rhythmically down her body, caressing her silken skin as if it belonged to him alone. With a soft sigh of complete submission, Gabbie slid her arms up around his neck, tipping her head back so that his mouth could take possession of that fluttering hollow in the base of her throat.

'Didn't I tell you fire could melt ice?' he murmured, his lips moving slowly back to hers and claiming them for his own once more, as his hand pressed into the small of her back, moulding her slender frame against his. With a groan, Gabbie felt her body arching against him of its own volition. She wanted him as she had never wanted any man before, it was an instinctive, unthinking reaction.

The roar of a motorcycle screeching to a halt on the loose gravel at the back of the cottage made them break apart. Involuntarily Gabbie gasped, putting a hand to her mouth. Whatever had come over her, behaving in such a wild, abandoned manner? She looked at Michael; his eyes were pools of desire, and his breathing was shallow and ragged.

'Hi, Gabbie—hi, Michael,' said Sam, breezing around the corner. 'I see you're all ready for the snorkelling, then, Gabbie.'

'I . . . oh yes,' said Gabbie, trying to collect her wits which had just been scattered to the four corners of the earth. 'I'll just slip on a pair of shorts and a tee-shirt and join you.' She picked up the towel which had fallen to the ground during her passionate embrace with Michael. She threw it at Sam. 'You can put this on the motorbike for me.'

With that, she scuttled up the stairs as fast as her legs would carry her, her heart still thumping like a crazy thing in her breast. Once in her bedroom, she stole across to the ancient peeling mirror and stared at her reflection, touching her lips as the memory of Michael's searing kiss flooded over her. Suddenly she shivered. If Sam hadn't arrived they would probably have ended up in bed—she would never have resisted, coherent thought hadn't been possible. Michael had just taken complete possession of her body and mind.

With a quick angry movement she turned away from the mirror, brushing her hair savagely and tying it back in a ponytail. She was a fool—there could be nothing between her and a man like Michael Nikolaides. Why, only yesterday he'd told her that he believed men and women had their designated places, and that men were the masters. By giving in to her own previously unsuspected primitive instincts, she had played right into his hands.

As she dressed she could near the two men talking on the patio below, and composing her features into a cool smile, joined them. Sam looked up and smiled. 'It seems our Medical Director had forgotten it was *his* Saturday afternoon on duty, not mine,' he said. 'Good job I turned up, isn't it?'

'A very good job,' said Gabbie, marvelling at the smooth assurance of her voice, 'but Michael was just going anyway. Come on!' Without waiting for a reply or looking in Michael's direction, she ran over to the motorbike and climbed on the pillion seat.

'See you later,' said Michael as he climbed into his car and started the engine.

'Oh no, you won't, Sam and I are going to a disco in Heraklion, and we shall be back terribly late!'

'Are we?' said Sam, slightly surprised. But the noise of the car engine drowned his words, and Gabbie was spared the need of an explanation in front of Michael.

CHAPTER SEVEN

SAM looked at Gabbie through narrowed eyes. 'I don't remember mentioning a disco,' he said, 'but . . .' he shrugged his shoulders and grinned, 'who am I to complain!'

'Oh, I . . . well, actually Michael had some idea of going over the Bokas case,' replied Gabbie, feeling the need to stretch the truth a little, 'and I felt I'd done enough work for one day—after all, it is my off-duty time, so I invented the disco.' She looked at Sam, biting her bottom lip anxiously. 'I hope you don't mind.'

'Of course not.' Sam's grin spread across his goodnatured face. 'I don't know why I didn't think of it myself. That's just what we'll do—eat first in Heraklion and then enjoy ourselves at a disco. There's a new one just opened called The Pink Parrot, and according to rumour their Pink Parrot cocktails are an absolute knockout!'

'Well, in that case, I shall definitely not allow you to drink one, if we're going on this thing.' Gabbie laughed, relieved that he'd taken it so well. They roared off down the winding road towards the sea, her hair streaming back in the wind blowing all thoughts of Michael away.

Sam took her to Elounda, a little village a few miles from Aghios Nikolaos, parking the motorbike near two derelict stone windmills, their once distinctive circular sails now only rotting wooden spokes. He told her they were going to dive on and around Olous.

'Olous?' queried Gabbie, struggling into the flippers Sam passed to her.

'A sunken city,' he told her. 'Of course, everything of real interest has been taken and put in the museum at Aghios Nikolaos, but you can still see the remains of the houses and streets, and some of the houses have beautiful mosaic floors.'

Never having snorkelled before, Gabbie listened carefully, and forgot completely about Michael and the shattering kiss. Sitting on the warm rocks, she put on her mask, and with some trepidation lowered herself into the tranquil sea. There was a gentle swell, nothing to worry about, Sam said, and Gabbie felt as if the sea was breathing, as she was gently lifted and then fell with the movement of the clear green water. Gripping the mouthpiece of the snorkel firmly between her teeth, she lowered her face into the sea.

It was a new silent world; minute particles of minerals glinted in the smooth sand of the bottom as they swam silently along, and soon Sam was pointing out the ruins they had come to see—stone walls, paved streets and mosaics depicting fishes and birds, a drowned city from long ago. Gabbie wondered about the people who had once lived there; it seemed eerie looking down on the remains of their world, almost as if they were prying into something private. After what seemed to Gabbie a

very short while, Sam indicated to her that they
should surface.

'We should get out now,' he said, as soon as their
heads were above water, 'you've been in quite a
long while for a novice.'

'Oh!' Gabbie protested, disappointed that it was
over so soon. 'I could go on for ever, and we've only
been . . .'

'We've been in the water for over an hour—
come on.' Sam would brook no argument and
hauled her out of the sea, to sit beside him on the
sunbaked rocks.

With a sigh of satisfaction at the warmth, she
realised she had been getting chilled without realising it. Removing her mask and flippers, she lay
back on the smooth surface of the rock, letting the
sun soak into her bones. She closed her eyes, trying
to visualise the sunken city again, but for some irritating reason Michael Nikolaides' face kept getting
in the way, and his eyes were glinting in a predatory
way, the look she'd seen in them not so long ago.
With a sigh she sat up, shaking her wet hair to dry it.

'Do you mind if I ask you something?' asked
Sam. He had lit a small cheroot and was blowing
perfect smoke rings into the still air.

'No, go ahead,' she leaned up on one elbow and
smiled, 'as long as it's not too personal!'

Sam drew deeply on his cheroot. 'Well,' he
drawled slowly, 'I guess you might think it is.'

'Oh, for goodness' sake get on with it,' said
Gabbie, putting on her no-nonsense practical
nurse's voice.

'I noticed you moved out of the villa as soon as Michael came back,' said Sam.

'Well, what of that? Maria had quite enough to cope with, without a visitor as well!'

'Oh, was that the reason? I thought perhaps it was because you'd fallen for Michael, like most of the other women who come into contact with him. I know I told you he was a misogynist, but that doesn't stop women falling for him like ninepins.'

Gabbie laughed. 'What an imagination! Have I given you any reason to suspect that I've fallen for Michael Nikolaides? Surely you must have heard that we've had several stand-up fights already?'

'Well, yes,' said Sam slowly, then he turned and looked at her. 'But I thought I detected an atmosphere between you two when I arrived.'

Gabbie swallowed hard, remembering that passionate kiss and her temporary—only temporary, she reminded herself fiercely—lapse of self-control. 'What you detected was hostility,' she said firmly. 'Michael Nikolaides is a male chauvinist of the first order in my book, I can't stand the man!'

'I see,' said Sam, raising his eyebrows with a grin. 'That's laying it on pretty strongly.'

'He's given me good reason to feel pretty strongly about it,' replied Gabbie with some asperity. 'But if he's such a knockout with women as you say, why isn't he married? After all, he's quite long in the tooth—thirty-six, I believe. He must have met *someone* he fancied, he can't have disliked them all!'

Sam roared with laughter. 'You call thirty-six

long in the tooth? Thanks a bundle! I'm thirty-four, although I suppose,' he added, pulling a rude face, 'to a mere twenty-six-year-old, the thirties must seem positively geriatric!'

'Oh Sam!' Gabbie clapped her hand to her mouth, aghast at her indiscretion. 'I didn't mean I thought *you* old!'

'I'm relieved to hear it,' said Sam. 'And anyway, apparently Michael was engaged once, a long time ago, to a local Greek girl. But she jilted him, ran off with some penniless English student she met while he was here on holiday. I've always felt that's why he's a little anti-English, or hadn't you noticed?'

Gabbie opened her blue eyes expressively. 'I've noticed! But at least it proves one thing,' she went on, 'Michael Nikolaides isn't everyone's cup of tea, at least one other female besides me has found him completely resistible!' But even as she spoke, she had to firmly suppress the thought that he wasn't so easy to resist, especially when he got too near.

In order to get the Greek doctor back where he belonged, at the very bottom of her list of least favourite men, she told Sam about the ructions with the Mayor, Mr Bokas. 'And Michael didn't even stand up for me. Not one word did he say!' she finished furiously.

'As a matter of fact I overheard him talking to that bully-boy Mr Bokas,' said Sam quietly. 'I'd just returned from Sitea. You're doing Michael a grave injustice if you think he didn't stand up for you—he most certainly did. He told Mr Bokas that you were the best nurse in the hospital, and that you'd saved his son's life. In fact he gave the wretch the telling off he deserved. But he had to do it in private, however—Mr Bokas *is* the Mayor, and Michael is sensitive enough to realise he needed to keep face in front of all the staff in the hospital. Mr Bokas, I mean, not Michael.'

'Oh,' said Gabbie, suddenly feeling very mean. Michael must have come to the cottage to tell her that, and she hadn't let him get a word in edgeways. She'd been rude and impatient, and then had ended up dissolving into his arms! He must think she belonged firmly in the category of 'mad dogs and Englishmen' or in her case 'women'. 'Oh dear,' she said again.

'I shouldn't worry about it,' said Sam comfortably, 'Michael has pretty broad shoulders, I doubt if he took offence.' He looked at the huge waterproof watch he was wearing. 'Come on, let's go and get cleaned up, then we'll eat and go to the Pink Parrot.'

The meal was nice, in a little fish restaurant high on the hill overlooking the Venetian fortress which guarded Heraklion harbour, but the Pink Parrot lived up to its name. It was noisy and crowded, and the house cocktail Sam insisted she drink left Gabbie with a throbbing headache and she was not sorry to get home.

Waving goodbye to Sam, she climbed wearily into bed. It had been a long day, one way and another. She was too tired, even, to eject Aphrodite, who took advantage of her weakened state to snuggle into bed with her.

'Well, just don't you dare have your babies tonight,' muttered Gabbie, before she turned over and fell into a deep sleep, during which she dreamed constantly of Michael. His face was floating along the drowned streets of Olous, constantly ebbing and flowing in the swell of the water.

Next morning evidence of the Pink Parrot cocktail still remained with her, in the form of a headache, so she took a leisurely breakfast of fruit juice and crusty bread, feeling very lazy as she sat on the lounger, admiring the view. Aphrodite felt more energetic, and frolicked about chasing butterflies.

'For an expectant mother, you've got no sense of propriety,' Gabbie reprimanded her, wondering when her family of one cat would be increased, and by how many. Ah well, she thought, eventually gathering up her breakfast things, in preparation to go down to the Nikolaides' villa, I'll cross that bridge when I come to it!

She arrived at the villa at about ten-thirty, just in time for coffee and biscuits. Maria was setting the tray under a huge yellow raffia umbrella. 'Michael is going to bring his father out on to the patio,' she said. 'I wonder if you would see if he needs any help.'

'Of course.' Gabbie was only too pleased to help Paulos, knowing he must be sick of the sight of the four walls of his bedroom. She started to make her way towards the bedroom, and bumped into Michael coming out from the kitchen.

She walked beside him down the long corridor

towards the room at the end of the villa where Paulos was. 'I've come to help with Paulos,' she said, feeling awkward. Then she paused and took a deep breath. 'And to apologise,' she added.

Michael stopped and looked at her, raising his dark brows, the expression in his eyes unreadable. 'Apologise?' he queried.

'Yes, about flying off the handle about Mr Bokas,' said Gabbie, studying the straps of her white sandals with sudden intensity. 'Sam told me you supported me—I thought you'd apologised for me. I'm sorry I didn't give you a chance to tell me.'

'Don't apologise,' said Michael, his voice throbbing with amusement. 'What happened later more than compensated!'

A sudden tight band constricted her throat, threatening to choke her, and Gabbie swallowed hard. 'I don't know what came over me,' she said, trying to keep her voice cool and matter-of-fact. 'I'm not usually so—so . . .' She ran out of breath as she desperately searched for the right word.

'Lustful,' suggested Michael wickedly.

Gabbie flashed him a look of pure ice from her sapphire eyes. 'That was *not* the word I was going to use! What happened was purely——' she paused, then said deliberately, 'purely a chemical or animal, call it what you will, reaction. Nothing more. I don't even particularly like you, Dr Nikolaides, and you don't like me.'

'Have it your way,' said Michael with a dismissive shrug. 'But,' he slipped an arm around

Gabbie's slender waist, 'you must admit it *was* nice, wasn't it!'

'I'm not admitting anything of the kind,' said Gabbie crossly, wriggling free from his restraining arm, glad that at that point they had reached Paulos' bedroom.

Between them they carefully helped Paulos, who was determined to do as much as possible for himself, into the wheelchair, then Michael pushed him out on to the patio.

'After coffee,' announced Paulos, 'I'm going to try to walk around the patio, using my walking frame.'

Michael looked worried. 'I've got to get back to the Institute,' he said, 'so . . .'

'I'll be here,' said Gabbie. 'Don't worry, between us, Maria and I will help.'

'I won't need any help,' said Paulos firmly, and Gabbie glanced at him, seeing for a moment the same determined lines in his face as those of his son.

'I know,' she smiled, 'of course you won't.'

Michael drank his coffee quickly, then left for the Institute, leaving Maria, Paulos and Gabbie sitting in the peaceful stillness of the garden. The only sound was the tinkling of the fountain at the end of the swimming pool and the constant whirring of the cicadas. A delicious smell of frying peppers and onions drifted out from the kitchen where Katy was preparing lunch.

Maria passed a letter to Gabbie which had arrived at the Institute; it was from Sue, and it made her remember her phone call to Peter. 'If I pay you may I make a call to England?' she asked Maria. 'I will time it so I know exactly how much to pay.'

'Of course, but we don't want you to pay!' Maria threw up her hands in horror at the very idea.

But Gabbie insisted. 'I'd prefer to,' she said, 'then I needn't be shy about asking when I need to use it.'

Maria nodded reluctantly, and Gabbie slit open her letter. In it Sue pleaded with her to try to talk to Peter, saying how much she missed him, that she loved him, but that he was being obstinate and wouldn't talk to her. Gabbie thought for a moment, then knew what she would do. She would ask Sue and Emma out as well as Peter, force them to talk.

After asking Maria's permission again, she made her way to the library to make her two telephone calls. She got through straight away to Peter, and told him she'd rented a cottage. 'It's lovely,' she said, omitting to mention the primitive facilities. 'It will do you good to have a holiday—you can sort yourself out, sort your thoughts out.'

She omitted to mention the fact, of course, that she intended to ask his wife and daughter out too, a few days later. She'd tell him that after she'd had a chance to actually talk to him face to face herself.

Peter demurred. 'I can't just up and go—we've got a locum to help out, it's true, but I'm not sure how good he is.'

'Probably very good,' said Gabbie firmly. 'You

should realise you can't cure all the ills of the world by yourself.'

'Well . . .' she could hear the hesitation in his voice, 'it *has* been raining an awful lot here. What's the weather like?'

'Blue skies, sunshine, absolutely perfect. Oh, come on, darling, please,' she used her most persuasive wheedling voice. 'In spite of the perfect weather I miss you. Come and stay with me for a couple of weeks—please, darling. It will do us both good.'

'Oh, all right, you've persuaded me,' Peter succumbed to his sister. 'I'll try and get a flight next Saturday.'

'Till next Saturday, then,' said Gabbie with a satisfied smile, softly replacing the receiver. All she had to do now was to get Sue and Emma to come over to Crete a few days later.

A sound from the doorway made her raise her head. Michael's huge frame, dressed in a crisp white coat, loomed in the doorway. Gabbie wondered how long he'd been standing there. 'Hasn't anyone ever told you it's rude to listen to other people's conversations?' she said crisply, to cover up the uneasy feeling of fluster his presence there caused.

'You certainly didn't waste time inviting your English boyfriend to visit,' he said, his lips curling. 'Is that who you're saving yourself for? Or will he get the same come-on, back-off signal as I got?'

'I didn't give you any come-on signal,' spluttered Gabbie, realising he'd heard her persuading Peter.

'And anyway, it's . . .'

'None of my business,' finished Michael for her. 'You're quite right.' Sticking his hands deep in the pockets of his white coat, he turned on his heel and walked quickly away.

For a moment Gabbie was tempted to run after him, to explain that it had been her brother she'd been calling, that she didn't have an English boy-friend, but then cool logic took over. What difference did it make what he thought anyway? She didn't like him, and if she took the trouble to explain, why then, he might even think she found him attractive! Which I don't, she told herself crossly, not at all; he is the most objectionable man on Crete—although on reflection she put Michael in second place, reserving the first place for the Mayor, Mr Bokas!

Collecting her thoughts together, she rang Sue, her sister-in-law, and using the same persuasive tone arranged for her to come over the following Wednesday. That would give her three whole days to talk some sense into Peter. If she couldn't do it in three days, then knowing her brother as well as she did, she knew she wouldn't be able to do it all.

After she'd made the second call and timed it, she went back to the patio and forced the correct amount of drachmas on a reluctant Maria. 'I can't,' the Greek woman protested, 'it's like taking money from my daughter!'

'You'll upset me terribly if you don't take it,' said Gabbie firmly, 'and then I'll feel I can't stay to lunch!'

'Oh dear, not you too!' wailed Maria. 'Michael has just announced that he won't be able to stay, although earlier this morning he said he would.' She looked at Gabbie pleadingly. 'Perhaps you could try to persuade him, Gabbie, I'm sure all that paperwork he says he's got can't be that urgent.'

'I doubt if I could persuade Michael to do anything,' said Gabbie truthfully.

Katy came staggering out with a great tray loaded with pieces of cheese, pistachio nuts and small fried pieces of octopus for starters. Paulos insisted on pouring out three very generous glasses of ouzo. His hand was shaky, but he managed it, and passed a glass to Gabbie.

'I think I shall sleep the whole afternoon,' said Gabbie, sipping the enormous ouzo. The glass was filled to the top with ice cubes and it made a very refreshing and very intoxicating drink.

'I do wish Michael would join us,' said Maria plaintively. 'He's been so bad-tempered lately—I can't think why.'

'Perhaps he is overworked,' suggested Paulos. 'Maybe we should get someone else to help out at the Institute.'

Gabbie had been about to agree. It was hard work for Sam and Michael, and although her presence helped a little, it was a drop in the ocean as far as they were concerned. As well as all the medical work, they also did the bulk of the administrative work which needed to be done by someone with medical experience. She had thought of offering to help, but had refrained, feeling that she still had to prove herself in Michael's eyes, even though Sam had told her that he had said she was the best nurse in the Institute. She opened her mouth to tell Paulos that she thought extra help would be a good idea, but the words were halted before they were ever uttered by the unexpected appearance of Michael.

He flopped down in the chair beside his father, not even glancing in Gabbie's direction, and poured himself an ouzo. 'I was just saying that perhaps you need an extra pair of hands,' said Paulos. 'You seem to be out of sorts—tired, perhaps.'

'Nonsense,' said Michael, 'I'm not tired. But I will admit,' his black eyes looked directly at Gabbie, who felt herself colouring beneath his gaze, 'that I did have a frustrating day yesterday!'

'Clear the table,' ordered Maria, bustling in by the side of Katy. 'We must eat the dolmades while they are fresh.'

Gabbie got to her feet, hastily removing the tray of bits and pieces. 'I'll carry this through to the kitchen,' she called, glad to get away from the unnerving, penetrating eyes opposite her. What a cheek he had, she fumed, making her way to the kitchen, he obviously didn't intend to let her forget the fact that she'd very nearly succumbed to his charms!

'Damn the man,' she said out loud, setting the tray down viciously. 'Damn, damn, damn you, Michael Nikolaides!'

CHAPTER EIGHT

MONDAY dawned as usual, the sea glistening under the arc of a perfect azure sky, not one tiny little cloud in sight. Gabbie drove down to the Institute humming happily. It was Michael's half day off, so at least she'd have one morning's peace. I really will have to get my nerves under control, she told herself fiercely, it's quite ridiculous letting one man put you on edge; it had never happened before, she reminded herself, it was totally illogical.

After her usual visit to Maria and Paulos, she breezed along to her office. The postman had already been, she noticed—that was a minor miracle in itself so early in the morning; then amongst the other mail she noticed a letter from England for her, in her mother's handwriting.

For a moment she hesitated. She had pushed all thoughts of her mother and her unpleasant suggestion back to the dark recesses of her mind ever since she'd been in Crete, and didn't particularly want to resurrect them again. But then, with a sigh, she opened it. She had to be sensible; it was no use pretending unpleasant things didn't happen, or didn't exist. However, as she read on, the brilliant sunshine of outside seemed to flood into her room. Her mother had written apologising, saying Gabbie had given her something to think about, and that she was right. She actually apologised and asked Gabbie to forgive her, and added that she had been in touch with Peter too, telling him not to make the same mistake as herself, letting stubborn bitter pride get in the way of real happiness. 'I know perhaps you will find it difficult to forgive me,' she had written, 'but I hope one day you will, and that also one day you will find true happiness with the right man, so that you can have the proper family life that was denied you as a child.'

Gabbie put the letter down slowly. 'Poor Mother,' she whispered, knowing how very difficult it must have been for her mother to admit that she had never given herself or Peter a family life. It was too late for her now, but it was not too late for Peter, and Gabbie tightened her lips as she thought with determination. By hook or by crook, Peter and Sue would get back together again, so that Emma, their daughter, could have a real family life, and not be shunted around as they had been as children.

She was still standing thinking of Peter and Sue, staring with unseeing eyes across the green expanse of the lawn, where Spyros was already busy with his hose watering the thirsty plants, when the door to her office burst open. Gabbie turned quickly—the last few times that it had happened it had meant an emergency, and one look at Michael's face told her that this was no exception.

'How's your midwifery?' he asked abruptly.

'Not bad. I did a refresher course in conjunction

with the neo-natal intensive care course only three months ago. Why?'

'You're going to need all your skills in both directions, I think,' said Michael. 'I can't remember the last time I did obstetrics.' Grabbing her arm unceremoniously, he dragged her off down the corridor. 'I know we're a paediatric hospital,' he said in answer to Gabbie's startled questioning expression, 'but a young girl from a mountain village, with her husband in tow, has just turned up on the doorstep in an advanced state of labour. I gather from them that it's premature, and from the size of her I think it's probably twins.'

'We've got two incubators free,' said Gabbie, her mind running on ahead to the various possible complications.

'The only two,' replied Michael grimly. 'Thank God we don't have to use them often—this way.' He turned the corridor and started down the long corridor towards the rooms next to Intensive Care and the operating theatres.

'I've got Sophie to take her through into theatre, we'll deliver her there, and then if all goes well we can keep her and the babies in the upper room, well away from any possible source of infection.'

Gabbie nodded. That was logical, and she said a little silent prayer that the babies would be healthy and not too premature, as she followed Michael into the spare operating theatre. She could see the young girl, looking very frightened and doubled up with contractions already on the couch; Sophie had had the presence of mind to put up the side safety walls, and the girl was clinging on to the metal rails, the whiteness of the bones of her knuckles showing through where she held on so tightly. Poor kid, thought Gabbie, she probably hasn't got a clue what's happening to her—no ante-natal care, no education.

She was right. 'They are mountain people,' whispered Sophie, 'they walked all night down from the highest village, because her grandmother said the baby was dead, but they didn't want to believe it. So they came here for help.'

Gabbie placed a soothing hand on the girl's brow, and gently prizing loose one of her hands held it tightly. Human contact was much more comforting than that of cold metal.

Michael bent over her, listening anxiously through his stethoscope as he moved it around on the girl's taut stomach. 'There are definitely two,' he said with a flicker of a smile, 'and they are both alive.'

'Oh, twins!' said Sophie excitedly, smiling broadly.

'Let's wait until they're both born safely before we congratulate ourselves,' said Michael, his face grim and drawn with worry.

Gabbie looked at him. His skin was swarthy at the best of times, but now, with the faint shadow of a beard where he hadn't had time to shave, and dark circles under his eyes, he looked almost like an Arab. By the look of him he must have been up all night.

His next words confirmed it. 'I could do without a

difficult delivery this morning, I've been with the Alexiou boy all night, had to admit him in the early hours of this morning.'

'What about Sam?' asked Gabbie, as gently she started undressing the girl and sponging her down with warm soap and water, then swabbed the vulval area extensively with hibitane.

'He's already started in theatre,' replied Michael briefly, 'and anyway, I'm not sure I'm up to operating this morning. This is probably the lesser of two evils.'

Sophie had taken the young husband outside. He was exhausted after the walk down the mountainside during the night, and needed something to eat and drink. As she gave the girl a sip of water, Gabbie marvelled at her resilience. She had walked miles, and was now about to deliver twins; Gabbie also knew the courage it must have taken to have ignored the family grandmother's pronounciation that the baby was dead and it was all a waste of time. Family tradition was strong in the mountain villages, it took exceptional will to stand up against someone as powerful as the maternal grandmother —that much Gabbie had leaned during her short stay in Crete.

It was her exceptional strength and willpower that kept the girl going, and enabled her to obey their commands, to breathe when told, and then later to push when told. Michael continued monitoring, and making manual examinations, while Gabbie tried to control the labour as best she could, to make it as easy as possible for the girl. She gave the instructions and Sophie translated, as they stood one each side of her, holding her hands, wiping her brow and generally comforting and encouraging her.

The second stage of labour started only about ten minutes after Sophie and Gabbie had finished washing the patient, whose name was Mrs Haidis.

She gave a sudden cry of fear as her membranes ruptured. 'Tell her not to be frightened,' said Gabbie urgently to Sophie, 'tell her it's right and natural for this to happen, and that soon she will have her babies. Everything will be all right.'

Sophie translated rapidly, and Michael muttered to Gabbie, 'I said she was in an advanced stage, but I didn't realise how advanced!'

Gabbie didn't reply, she was too busy checking the quantity and colour of the liquid. All seemed normal, then she checked the blood pressure, normal too. After that she quickly checked the incubators; they were warm and ready lined with sterile cotton blankets. They had no sterile obstetric delivery packs in the Institute, so she had improvised, using sterile dressing packs from theatre, and now she and Michael scrubbed up and put on the sterile gloves, while Sophie gently helped Mrs Haidis over on to her left lateral side to ease the delivery.

In the event, the delivery went extremely smoothly considering the lack of ante-natal care, and the exhausted state of the mother before she had even started. The first baby's head presented, then slid out smoothly, Mrs Haidis panting obediently when told to. Without a word Michael passed the baby to Gabbie, who sucked out the mouth and nostrils using a sterile mucus catheter, which luckily they kept at the Institute for use on any very small babies who might be patients, then she placed the now healthily bawling but very small infant in the incubator.

She heard Michael speaking gently to Mrs Haidis, and had by now picked up enough Greek to know that he was telling her she had a son. A pleased smile spread across her face for a second, only to be replaced by a look of concentration as the desire to push down came again.

The second twin, another boy, was delivered uneventfully too, but he was smaller and cyanosed at the extremities, and at the same time Mrs Haidis began to bleed a little. Gabbie took the baby; from the look on Michael's face she knew he was worried that perhaps the placenta might have torn, and then they would have a major problem—a retained placenta and no instruments with which to remove it.

Quickly she aspirated the mucus from the baby's nose and mouth and applied an oxygen mask to deliver much-needed oxygen. To her intense relief the baby began to wriggle and turn pink. Small as he might be, he had strength, more than she had at first thought.

While Gabbie had been working on the baby, Michael had clamped the cords at the placental end, marking each one, indicating which baby it belonged to. At that time they were unsure whether the twins were uniovular or biovular.

'Let her rest for a moment now,' he said to Sophie. 'The bleeding has eased, we'll just keep our fingers crossed that she expels the placenta or placentae whole.'

Sophie spoke to Mrs Haidis, who by now was looking over anxiously at her babies in the incubators. Gabbie looked at Michael. 'I think it's all right for her to hold them for a few moments,' she said. 'They're not shocked. I was a little worried about the second one, but a burst of oxygen was all he needed.'

Michael nodded, looking pleased, then Mr Haidis was called in, having already been gowned and masked in readiness by Eleni outside. He stood by his wife's side, and together they held the twins, one after the other, then the babies were carefully put back into their incubators, where they fell peacefully asleep. They look like little skinny pink rabbits, thought Gabbie.

'Ideally we should have some ergometrine,' said Michael, sounding slightly worried. 'It's going to be a large placenta.'

'Don't worry,' said Gabbie, 'I have a feeling she's going to be all right—she's one of the healthiest and most co-operative mothers I've seen.' As she spoke she showed him the blood pressure chart Sophie had been keeping, then watching Michael gently press above the symphysis pubis and upwards. The cords receded a little into the vagina, a sign that the placenta was still attached to the uterine wall.

'I'll give her five minutes,' said Michael, 'and then I'll try manual removal by traction.'

'I don't think that would be a good idea,' Gabbie heard herself speaking before she could stop herself. But Michael had admitted earlier that it had been ages since he had delivered any babies, and she'd done her stint only three months ago. 'Everything has gone to plan so far,' she said, 'and has been perfectly normal. Interference with the third stage in a physiological event merits very serious consideration. Why hurry a normal event? There's no reason to suspect anything amiss—let's wait and see.'

She could see Sophie's face looking slightly surprised. The mere thought of a nurse telling a doctor what to do was a radical event as far as she was concerned. Gabbie swallowed hard, and hoped Michael wouldn't take offence, but she had to state her opinion, and felt like adding that she was fresher and in a better state of mind to make a more reasoned judgment than he. His face was now pallid with exhaustion, the strain of losing a night's sleep, and then a worrying delivery was telling.

'You're probably right,' was all he said, and he sat down in a chair beside Mrs Haidis. He patted her hand and said something in Greek, and Gabbie raised her eyebrows questioningly. 'I just told her to let us know when she wants to push again,' he said.

They didn't have to wait even five minutes. After about four, with just two well controlled pushes, the placentae were expelled together, membranes intact, followed by very little bleeding from the vagina. Just what would be expected normally.

Gabbie smiled happily. 'You see,' she said, 'I was right!' She didn't mean to crow, she was just pleased for both Mrs Haidis and Michael.

'I should have known you would be,' was Michael's reply, and Gabbie felt a little stab of hurt. No word of thanks for her help and common sense, when he had been in danger of making the wrong decision.

After making sure both mother and babies were settled, Michael left. 'I'll leave you to organise someone to stay with her for this morning, and arrange accommodation for the husband. We'll keep the babies in the incubators for the time being, though, as they're on the small side.'

After he had left Gabbie told Sophie to fetch Eleni, who next to Sophie she considered to be the most experienced nurse they had at the Institute. Someone with common sense and experience of neo-nates was really needed. Eleni had plenty of common sense, although she lacked neo-natal experience, as they all did. Still, she was a good nurse, and Gabbie couldn't foresee any problems. She instructed Eleni on the care of the babies in the incubators, and told her to let the mother try putting them to the breast to suck after she had rested a few hours, then Gabbie and Sophie left for a well-earned coffee.

They made their way down to the *kafénion* feeling they deserved their coffee. 'I'll get it,' said Sophie, 'you worked harder than I did.' Gabbie didn't protest, and left her making her way across to the counter. Once there, Gabbie could hear her chattering away to Olga, the elderly lady who served the food. She smiled—probably Sophie was telling her all about their surprise delivery of twins.

Sophie came back with two coffees and two pastries. '*Tiropittes*,' she said, 'a present from Olga for our good work!' She sank her teeth into one of the three-cornered puff pastry cheese pies with relish. 'Wasn't Michael marvellous?' she said, through a mouthful of pie.

'He did a good job,' replied Gabbie cautiously. She could hardly say that he'd been marvellous. Efficient, compassionate and hardworking, yes, but not marvellous.

'But anyway,' went on Sophie, a dreamy look coming into her eyes as she leaned back in the shade of the bamboo covering of the roof; they were sitting in the outside part of the *kafénion*, 'I've always thought he was. I hope he doesn't mind us taking a little break.'

'I should hope not indeed,' said Gabbie. 'Why on earth should he anyway? I think we deserve it.' She looked at Sophie curiously. 'Am I mistaken, or do you regard our Medical Director in a romantic light? Sam told me most of the girls fall for him.'

'Oh yes,' breathed Sophie, 'we all think he's gorgeous!' She sighed. 'If only he would look at *me* as a woman, and not just as a nurse!'

'You're welcome to him,' said Gabbie acidly. 'Michael Nikolaides leaves me completely cold, he's not my type at all. I like my men to be gentle and subtle, not aggressive and bullish, like . . . like some great steamroller!'

A loud cough behind her nearly caused her to choke on the remains of her *tiropitte*. She'd have recognised that cough anywhere, it was Michael, and, scarlet in the face from choking on the pastry and embarrassment, she wondered how much of the conversation he had overheard.

But to her relief he appeared to have heard nothing, as he made no comment other than to remark, 'I should have given these to you last week, it's the new work rotas for you and Sister Grant.'

'Sister Grant?' she queried.

'Yes, I've engaged another English Sister experienced in paediatrics. She will be arriving tomorrow.' He turned abruptly on his heel and walked away in the direction of the villa.

'Going for some well-earned sleep, I suppose,' said Sophie with a sympathetic smile, looking at his broad shoulders as he strode across the lawn that separated the villa from the Institute.

Gabbie said nothing; she was staring down at the papers he had just thrust into her hands. The name, typed in capitals, FELICITY GRANT, stared back up at her. He had engaged another Sister without even having the courtesy to bother to mention it to her! Her description of him being like a steamroller hadn't been exaggerated, she thought furiously, in fact it was very apt, that was exactly what he was. He just steamrollered on, regardless of anyone!

She wondered whether he had even told his father. Probably not, she thought, her mouth tightening with anger, otherwise *he* would have been certain to have mentioned it.

'You see what I mean,' she said, slamming the papers down furiously on the table, 'about him being like a steamroller!' She spat the word out. 'He's just engaged someone else, without even telling me—I suppose he hasn't got the courage to tell me he isn't satisfied with my work.'

'Oh, I'm sure it's not that. In fact I know it isn't,' Sophie stated to try to pacify her. 'I'm sure it's because he thinks you are overworked. He is concerned about you, I expect.'

'Concerned about me!' Gabbie's voice rose to an indignant squeak as she tried to refrain from speaking too loudly, not wanting other staff sitting around them to hear. 'Oh yes, he's so concerned that if I dropped dead in my tracks, he'd merely step over the body and advertise for an immediate replacement!'

Sophie giggled at Gabbie's pink-faced, furious expression, 'Oh, you do get hot under the collar,' she said, using one of Sam's expressions, 'and for a ice maiden too!'

That phrase rang an ominously familiar bell. 'What exactly do you mean by that expression?' demanded Gabbie, pinning Sophie down with a glare that had her wriggling uncomfortably in her seat.

'Well . . .' Sophie was clearly embarrassed now.

'Go on,' said Gabbie, 'I'm interested to know what prompted you to use that particular expression.'

'Well,' said Sophie again, then took a deep breath and gabbled, 'Sam told me that Michael asked him how he was getting along with you, were there any romantic inclinations, and Sam said no, you and he were just platonic friends. Then apparently Michael said he wasn't surprised, that you were an ice maiden in looks and temperament.'

'Oh, he did, did he?' said Gabbie through gritted teeth. 'Well, he may have an unpleasant surprise when he discovers just how icy this ice maiden can be!'

'Oh, Gabbie, please don't say anything,' pleaded Sophie. 'I'm sure he only meant it as a joke, and you'll get me into trouble. Sam will know it was me—you know what I'm like for blurting things out!'

Gabbie looked at the sheaf of papers on the table in front of her, and sighed. There was not much she could do, and she didn't want to get Sophie into trouble. The appointment of the new Sister was a fait accompli. She only hoped that she would like her, and they'd get on well together. Anyway, she consoled herself, Peter and Sue are arriving next week, so at least with the new rotas I should get a little more time off duty.

Perhaps Michael really had had her welfare at heart, but at least he could have told her, maybe even have asked her advice. But no, on second thoughts, he would never do that. He was the master and she the servant, he'd made that plain on several occasions!

He would run the Institute the way *he* thought,

and he certainly wouldn't dream of asking advice from a Sister whose appointment he hadn't even approved. The thought made Gabbie feel miserable, casting a blight over the day; he must have approved the appointment of the new Sister as he'd made it himself, although she wondered how and when he had actually appointed her, as he hadn't left the island since he arrived back to take charge of the Institute.

She was soon to find out when she sat with Sam at lunchtime. 'Hi,' he said, joining her at her table. 'I gather Michael has told you.'

'About the new Sister, you mean?' said Gabbie glumly. Even the fact that Mrs Haidis and the twins were doing spendidly had failed to cheer her up.

'Don't look so gloomy—it's going to ease the work-load, especially for you.'

'Tell me something,' it was the question Gabbie had been dying to ask, 'how did he find her? How did he appoint her? He hasn't been to England.'

'Oh, I understand she's an old friend. They met in the States some years ago, and she and Michael have corresponded regularly ever since. She hasn't been working in England recently, but in Denver, Colorado, and that's where Michael asked her to come over, when he knew his father had been taken ill.'

'Why didn't he mention it before?'

'I suppose he was waiting for all the paperwork to be sorted out—she had to give in her notice to leave her job in the States, you know how it is,' said Sam. He seemed completely unconcerned, as if it was the most natural thing in the world.

'I think he didn't want me to know,' persisted Gabbie. 'He's never approved of my appointment, you know.'

'Oh, come on, Gabbie, you're getting paranoid about the guy! I know Michael, he always springs surprises like this, he keeps his own counsel until everything is finalised.' Sam glanced at his watch and jumped up. 'Got a mixed outpatient session this afternoon—must dash.' He put a friendly hand on Gabbie's shoulder and squeezed it. 'Michael likes you, take my word for it.'

'Huh,' said Gabbie, trying to smile. 'I suppose I'll have to.' But all the same she couldn't dispel the feeling of irritation mixed with hurt pride. It was the fact that Michael hadn't even thought it necessary to mention it to her that really hurt.

CHAPTER NINE

FELICITY GRANT duly arrived the following day, and Gabbie found herself being introduced by Michael to a small, dark, pretty girl. She was as petite and vivacious as Gabbie was tall, fair and quiet—babbling over with enthusiasm about the Institute, Crete and Michael, who, she told Gabbie, she had known for simply 'yonks'.

'I gather the work-load has been pretty heavy,' she said, looking around Gabbie's office, 'and I also understand we've got to share the office—I'm sorry about that, I'll try not to get in your way.'

Gabbie had also been told that fact by Michael that morning, when she had been at the villa visiting Paulos. She said nothing, merely nodded, but couldn't help feeling it was just another example of the fact that he didn't really want her there at all, because he had never approved of her. She wished vehemently with all her heart, at that moment, that she could give in her notice and tell the tall arrogant man who was towering above her to get lost! But she had given her word to Paulos and couldn't bring herself to break her promise. I must keep my word, for the time being at least, she told herself. But she had to admit that there was another reason; gradually she had succumbed to the magic of Crete, the sunshine, her little cottage on the mountain-

side, and now she had the added responsibility of
Aphrodite—who would look after her if she went
away?

Felicity pushed a pile of suitcases over into the
corner of the office. 'Sorry about these,' she apologised. 'I'll get them out of your way just as soon as
I've organised some accommodation.'

'You're not staying at the villa, then?'

Felicity shook her head. 'Michael's mother did
invite me, but I felt it would be too inhibiting living
with one's boss. Anyway, I'm used to sharing
with other girls, free to wash my hair when I like,
or lounge around and be as untidy as I want to
be—it's ages since I've had to fit in with a family
routine.'

'Well, if you like,' Gabbie heard herself saying, 'I
rent a small cottage a few kilometres from here. It's
on the mountainside overlooking the bay, the view
is wonderful, although the amenities are a bit basic.
I don't mind sharing, and you can always look
around and rent somewhere else later, if you prefer
to be on your own.'

'Whew, that's great!' said Felicity with a huge
sigh of relief. 'To tell you the truth, I was
wondering if I'd have a roof over my head tonight!'

In spite of herself, Gabbie found she liked
Felicity. There was an open friendliness about her
which was disarming, and she grinned, wondering
what Sam would think of her, although she had a
pretty good idea. He would make a pass at the first
available opportunity, unless of course Michael got
in first! She glanced at Felicity, who was busy

studying the map of Crete on the wall, and wondered if there was anything between her and Michael. She *was* very attractive, a dark prettiness that would turn any man's head.

She lent Felicity her car, and gave her instructions on how to get to the cottage. 'Oh, by the way, there's one other occupant,' she said, 'a small pregnant cat I've adopted.'

'When are we going to be step-parents?' asked Felicity, lugging her cases through the door.

Gabbie laughed. 'According to Michael, any day now.' Yes, she definitely liked Felicity, in fact it would be quite nice sharing, having someone to gossip with. It would also be the perfect excuse to pack Peter and Sue off to a hotel for a reconciliation—she'd ask Felicity if she would mind helping her keep an eye on young Emma; instinctively, though, she knew she wouldn't mind at all; she had an easygoing air about her.

She was right. Felicity didn't mind, and was very sympathetic when Gabbie explained to her how she was scheming to get her stubborn brother and his wife back together again.

'I'm lucky,' said Felicity, sitting with Aphrodite purring on her lap, that evening; it was quite late and they were sitting out, sharing a bottle of wine. 'My parents were and still are very happily married. I come from a family of six, I have three brothers and two sisters, all scattered now around the world, but we all go home regularly. It's the centre of our world, no matter where any of us are.'

Gabbie envied her. No wonder she was so easy-going, so self-confident. She was also much more domesticated than Gabbie, and as time went on nagged her into making the cottage a little less primitive. Whenever she had time off, she foraged around Heraklion, with its maze of little back streets that sold everything imaginable, always coming back with something for the cottage, even installing a battery-operated electric light in the loo, but her 'pièce de résistance' was the day she came back with a secondhand mahogany wooden loo seat.

'I'm tired of getting splinters in my rear end,' she announced firmly to an astonished Gabbie. 'I'm going to fix this thing and make life more comfortable!'

When she had finished, both girls spent some time inspecting and admiring her handiwork. Gabbie did her share, polishing the wood till it gleamed red, and she also polished the brass handle that pulled the lid down, until she could see her reflection in it.

As they stood there admiring it, Gabbie suddenly laughed. 'If anyone had told me this time last year that the highlight of one of my days would be a wooden loo seat, I would never have believed them!'

'I would have done,' said Felicity with a grin. 'I forgot to tell you that my mum and dad live in the country, and when I was little we had an outside privy. It's only in the last few years that my parents have made any concessions to the twentieth century by having a flush toilet built on to the house.'

'That accounts for your practical nature, then,' said Gabbie. 'I'm afraid I've always had all the mod cons.'

Although she had originally been annoyed at Michael appointing another Sister, Gabbie had to admit, albeit reluctantly at first, that the new rota worked very well indeed. Not only did it give her more time off, but it also left her much more time for teaching, so that she was able to organise two sessions a week, splitting each group into smaller groups. In turn, this made organising the ward and theatre rotas much easier, and enabled her to have a more intimate relationship with the girls she was teaching.

Felicity had been quite adamant about the teaching. 'Michael says you're very good,' she said, 'and I know I'm not. I'm the practical kind—put me in front of a group of people and tell me to explain something, I just get tongue-tied, everything comes out all wrong!'

So Gabbie happily let Felicity take a slightly greater share of the clinical work-load, and also some of the administrative burden from Sam and Michael, while she concentrated on scaling up her programme of teaching. It meant that she saw less of Michael, and that suited her; or at least she told herself it did, but for some strange reason she missed their verbal sparring.

Her first week of sharing with Felicity had almost gone, time had passed so quickly Gabbie wondered where on earth the week had disappeared to. Next day was the Saturday of Peter's arrival, and she had to set off early to meet him at the airport. Although, as Felicity had said, it hardly seemed worthwhile arriving on time, it was very rare for one of the flights to do the same!

Felicity had by now hired a car of her own, and that morning had decided to go on earlier to the Institute, at the unearthly hour of five o'clock. She was worried about the Alexiou boy, who was still an in-patient.

'Apparently Sotiris has never been as bad as he is this summer,' she told Gabbie. 'Michael is thinking of sending him to Athens, to a specialist there.'

Gabbie nodded. 'I know, you feel so helpless nursing asthmatics, there seems to be so little one can do to help. All the measures are only short-term.'

She thought of the little boy in his bed by the window, a pale little wraith who looked as if a puff of wind might blow him away. 'Probably his best chance *is* with a specialist,' she said. 'Not that Michael and Sam aren't doing a good job, but maybe a specialist could track down whatever it is that he's allergic to. The tests are very sophisticated now—in London I know we found some of the kids were allergic to the strangest things.'

Felicity looked concerned. 'I hope he does go to Athens.' Then her face brightened. 'Perhaps I could persuade Michael to let me fly with him in the ambulance plane, then I could do a bit of sight-seeing while I'm there.'

'Can you really imagine Michael allowing the ambulance plane to wait while you climbed the Acropolis?' asked Gabbie, raising her eyebrows.

Felicity laughed. 'Come to think of it, no,' she agreed. 'He believes in work, work and . . .'

'More work,' finished Gabbie as Felicity charged out of the doorway, nearly tripping over Aphrodite in the process. 'Mind out!' shouted Gabbie after her retreating heels. 'You might bring on premature labour!'

'Chance would be a fine thing!' Felicity shouted back, climbing into her car. 'That cat is putting off motherhood for as long as possible, I don't think she's got a maternal instinct in her!'

Watching the little tortoiseshell cat, her pregnancy now very obvious, chasing a pebble like a football across the patio outside the kitchen, Gabbie was inclined to agree. Half an hour after Felicity, she left too, pausing a moment to pat Aphrodite's little round head, before getting into her car and driving down to the Institute; as always making her morning call on Paulos and Maria.

Maria was in the bedroom when she arrived, arguing with Paulos who was sitting half dressed on the side of the bed. 'Oh, Gabbie,' she said, her voice full of relief at the sight of her, 'will you please tell him he's not to go over to the Institute?'

'Well, I don't think perhaps it's such a good idea just yet,' said Gabbie hesitantly, choosing her words with care. Paulos had a very obstinate set to his mouth, and looked pretty determined. 'Has Michael suggested it, then?'

'That's the whole point, Michael hasn't suggested anything,' snapped Paulos, his speech fully recovered by now. 'In fact he's done nothing but bite my head off these past few days, he's like a bear with a sore head!'

'That's true,' said Maria miserably, 'he has been very bad-tempered.'

'Something is wrong over there,' said Paulos, struggling into his shirt determinedly, 'and I'm going to see what it is.'

'Paulos, please!' Gabbie put a restraining hand on his arm. 'There's nothing wrong at the Institute, believe me.'

Paulos looked at her uncertainly. 'Are you sure?' he asked.

'Of course I'm sure, and I know Michael would tell you if there was anything, I'm sure he would.'

'He didn't tell me about that new Sister he appointed,' grumbled Paulos. 'Didn't want me to worry, he said, only told me afterwards.'

'He didn't tell me either,' said Gabbie, feeling a disgruntled stab of ill-will towards Michael for a moment, then her better nature triumphed and she said, 'Sam was probably right, he thought we were overworked, but waited until all the paperwork was sorted out, then just forgot to tell any of us.'

'You didn't tell me you were overworked,' said Paulos accusingly.

'I didn't think I was,' said Gabbie honestly. 'Hardworked, yes, but not overworked.' She laughed. 'I'm used to hard work, but I must admit the appointment of Felicity was a good idea. I've been able to plan a lot of extra teaching—you'll soon have the best trained paediatric nurses in Crete.'

'In Greece,' said a voice from the doorway.

Gabbie wheeled around. Michael's dark shape filled the doorway, silhouetted against the pale cream of the wall behind him; suddenly, without warning, her heart lurched so violently, she almost hiccuped.

'That must say something for your teaching,' she heard Paulos's voice say in the distance, as if from another planet.

For a few strange, unrealistic seconds, Gabbie stared at Michael, her eyes locked with his. She felt as if they were both in another world, far away from anyone else, and that her heart was in imminent danger of exploding.

Then the spell was broken as she heard Michael saying coolly, 'Yes, she is an excellent teacher.'

Tugging her eyes away from his, Gabbie turned back to Paulos. 'Now you can ask him yourself,' she said.

'Ask me what?' To her consternation Michael came over and stood beside her, his sleeve brushed against her arm, and Gabbie shivered as if she were cold, even though the brief touch seemed to sear her skin with a strange heat.

'Paulos is under the misapprehension that something is wrong at the Institute,' mumbled Gabbie, wishing she could stop feeling like some gauche teenager. It was those damned eyes of his, she told herself, perhaps he practised hypnosis!

'Something wrong at the Institute?' Michael's voice rose on a note of disbelief.

'I told him there was absolutely nothing to worry about, but . . .'

'It's all your fault, Michael,' interrupted Maria accusingly, 'worrying your father and me,' she added, 'being so bad-tempered, so moody.'

'Have I?' he said, then he turned to Gabbie. 'Is that what they're saying at the Institute too?'

Gabbie shrugged her shoulders. 'I don't know, I don't discuss you with anyone,' she said, which was quite true, 'and personally, as I haven't seen much of you this past week, I couldn't possibly say.'

'There you are, Father,' said Michael, suddenly switching on one of his charming smiles which even worked on his own father, thought Gabbie, watching in bemusement. 'Take Gabbie's word for it, if not mine. I am not bad-tempered, I am my usual charming, lovable self!'

'That's not exactly what I said,' protested Gabbie later, as they walked away from the villa together towards the Institute, leaving a happily reassured Paulos.

'Why have you been avoiding me?' Michael ignored her remark.

'Avoiding you? Why, I haven't. I've been busy, and so have you, it's just that our paths haven't crossed. I certainly haven't been avoiding you— why should I?'

'Because you're still annoyed at me for appointing Sister Grant without mentioning it to you.'

'Damn Sam and that big mouth of his!' said Gabbie crossly.

'Well, are you?'

'I was annoyed,' admitted Gabbie, 'but I'm not so childish as to bear grudges, and anyway, I have to acknowledge now that the new system is working very well. It gives me more time for teaching, and apart from that, it seems I wasn't the only person you didn't tell . . .'

Michael pulled a face. 'I forgot to tell just about everyone,' he admitted, then he continued, 'But I've noticed that you've taken some of the time allocated as "off-duty" and used it to teach. That time was meant for you to relax.'

'I have enough time off—the extra you've given me is too much, I prefer to work,' said Gabbie.

'You know what they say, all work and no play makes Jill a dull girl.'

'I was always taught that it made Jack a dull boy!' retorted Gabbie, adding, 'Maybe it's *you* who needs the time off. Your mother did say you've been very bad-tempered lately.'

'Yes,' said Michael, stopping suddenly in the middle of the lawn, 'I do need some relaxation. I need feminine company and an amusing evening, and . . .'

'Why don't you ask Felicity?' said Gabbie quickly. Instinct told her he was about to ask *her*, and illogically she stubbornly forestalled him. 'I need an early night, I've got to be at Heraklion airport at the crack of dawn to pick up my visitor.'

'Oh yes,' Michael's voice suddenly hardened

with disapproval, 'I was wondering when *he* was coming. But won't it cramp your style a little, now that Felicity's sharing the cottage?'

'Oh, no,' Gabbie couldn't resist saying, 'Felicity's *very* broadminded! 'Byee!' She marched ahead, leaving him still standing in the middle of the lawn; let him think what he likes, she thought obstinately.

The day passed quickly, but although she was busy, working in the wards in the morning, as Felicity had flown off to Athens with Sotiris Alexiou earlier in the day and was due back in the afternoon, Gabbie found she couldn't stop herself thinking about Michael. His dark face seemed to loom up in front of her whatever she was doing, and that afternoon, during the teaching session, she lost her place several times. In the end she gave up and dismissed the girls early. The meeting with Michael that morning had unnerved her. I must have missed him more than I thought, she mused, a conclusion which didn't make her feel at all happy.

When she got back to the cottage, Felicity was already there, having driven straight up after arriving back from Athens. She was drooling over Aphrodite, who had given birth during the day to just one adorable ginger kitten. She had ensconced her in a card board box on one of Gabbie's best cardigans in the corner of the kitchen, food and milk beside her so that she didn't have far to stir.

'The maternity ward,' said Felicity, putting her finger to her lips. 'Shush, she's asleep.'

'Couldn't you have given her an older cardigan,

preferably one of yours?' asked Gabbie; she could see at a glance that the pale lemon one with the pearls buttons would never be fit to wear again.

'I was in a rush—I'm going out with Michael tonight, and I had to get her settled, poor little lamb. Anyway,' added Felicity with an indisputable logic, 'she is your cat.'

The kitten, his head about the size of a large gooseberry, suckled, and Aphrodite gave a contented purr, snuggling her forepaws protectively around her baby. Gabbie smiled; oh well, what was a cardigan anyway!

'By the way,' said Felicity, rushing upstairs with a bowl of hot water, to wash in the privacy of her bedroom, 'how is the maternity ward at the Institute? That's the one place I haven't been to since I arrived.'

'Oh, Mrs Haidis is fine,' said Gabbie, who had popped in every day since the delivery, although the nursing care had been taken over by Eleni and one of the other nurses, everything being straightforward. 'The babies are out of the incubators, it's just a question of waiting until they reach three and a half kilogrammes, then she can take them back to the village. I think she'll manage fine, and there's always the extended family system of the village to help her.'

'Good.' Felicity disappeared into her bedroom, and Gabbie heard the water sploshing about; that was really the only thing they could have done with, a bath. Then she smiled to herself. Knowing Felicity, the next time she went shopping she'd probably buy a tin one and bring it back!

Pouring herself a glass of cool lemonade—a Calor gas fridge was another one of their newly acquired luxuries—she wandered out on to the patio and stood, glass in hand, idly looking down across at the view. The sea shone like a sheet of hammered gold under the setting sun, all was peace and quiet, except for the sound of a car engine as it wound its way up the mountain road.

'That'll be Michael,' Felicity shouted down the stairs. 'Keep him amused, will you, I'm not ready yet.'

Keeping Michael amused was the last thing Gabbie wanted to do, but she forced herself to smile and offer him a drink, which he declined, when he arrived. They stood in awkward silence side by side on the patio, both looking at the sunset, then Gabbie stole a surreptitious sideways glance. His profile was positively hawklike, and his dark hair had grown and really needed trimming, it was curling thickly over the edge of his impeccably white collar. Gabbie felt an impulsive, almost irresistible urge to run her fingers through it; there was something compelling attractive about his whole appearance. Quite suddenly she felt hollow inside, and wished it was her, not Felicity, that he was escorting that evening. But her own stubbornness had prevented that. And a good thing too, she told herself, dragging her eyes away from Michael and trying to concentrate on the view; the very last thing you want to do is to start getting weak at the

knees and soppy about your boss. He's a misogynist, she reminded herself, Sam says so, he likes
women, but he never loves them; and anyway, she
had no desire to become emotionally involved with
anyone, in spite of her mother's wishes for her
happiness.

'You could always come with us if you've nothing
better to do,' Michael's voice suddenly broke into
her thoughts. The invitation surprised her.

'Oh no,' Gabbie said quickly, finding she was
breathless as he moved a step closer. 'You know
what they say, two's company, three's a crowd . . .'
Her voice tailed off as she made the mistake of
glancing up at him and letting her gaze be caught by
his. She had the same feeling she had experienced
that morning, that they were completely alone,
only the two of them. Her heart began to thud,
slamming against her rib-cage like an imprisoned
thing trying to get out.

She could feel his warm breath fanning her
cheek. 'Gabbie,' he said, 'I . . .' then the next
moment she was in his arms, his mouth was on hers
and she was drowning in a sea of longing. Longing
never to be set free, to stay in his arms for ever, as a
feeling of warmth and strength suddenly swept over
her. She kissed him back, her unspoken longing
surfacing, she forgot about Felicity, about everything except the exquisite sensation of being held
close to that hard body that told her he needed her
as much as she wanted him.

'Won't be a minute. Has Gabbie shown you our
new family?' Felicity's voice floating down the

stairs made them break abruptly apart.

For a moment they remained staring, neither speaking. Then, feeling two bright spots of colour flaring in her cheeks, Gabbie turned away hurriedly; she'd done it again, let herself be captivated by sheer animal instinct—there was no other explanation. It seemed she was totally out of control when Michael got near her.

'Aphrodite's had her kitten,' she said, attempting to drag herself back down on to the plane of sanity.

But before Michael could speak, Felicity clattered down the stairs, looking very pretty in a bright red sun-dress with matching shawl. 'Let's go,' she said happily, 'I'm starving!'

They left without Michael saying another word to Gabbie, and she watched the car disappear down the road away from the cottage with a heart that felt like a lump of lead in her chest. Why, oh, why had she been so stupid and obstinate? If she hadn't, it might have been her sitting beside him in the car, but in her heart of hearts she knew why. She was afraid of getting involved with Michael, afraid of getting hurt, afraid of the strength of feeling he generated whenever he even got near her. How can I feel the way I do when I'm in his arms, she asked herself miserably, when other times we quarrel ferociously?

She went to bed that night still haunted by the question, to which there seemed no logical answer. How could she feel such a passionate longing for a man she didn't even like? Perhaps she'd fallen in love with him, the thought came suddenly, completely unbidden; love and hate were always said to be closely akin. Rubbish, she told herself firmly; how could I love him? Apart from not liking him I don't even known him very well; but all the same it was an uncomfortable thought that prevented her from sleeping for hours.

Eventually she drifted off into a confused unhappy sleep, only to be awakened by the sound of Felicity's laughter and Michael's low voice. They had arrived back—looking at the luminous dial of her watch she saw that it was three in the morning; unhappily she buried her head in the pillow and tried not to think about what they might have been doing all that time.

CHAPTER TEN

FELICITY was still asleep when Gabbie left the cottage to drive to Heraklion airport the following morning. She was glad—it meant she didn't have to ask her if she'd enjoyed her evening with Michael. Not that I'm interested, she told herself without much conviction! She bit her lips at the very thought, as she hastily swallowed a cup of instant coffee. Why did life have to be so complicated? All her life she had thought she had known precisely where she was going, no emotional hang-ups for her, a career and a well-ordered life, that had been her ambition, and one she had successfully achieved. But with the sudden closure of the paediatric hospital in London, she been precipitated into taking a job abroad; then with Paulos' illness she had been precipitated again, quite against her own volition, into close contact with a very disturbing man.

'Oh dear, what shall I do?' she said softly, stroking Aphrodite before she left, but she was no help. She merely lolled back contentedly in the cardboard box, looking up at Gabbie with great yellow eyes.

Perhaps Peter's teasing about her having Freudian desires for children of her own had something to do with it, she thought; maybe subconsciously she did want what most other girls want, a husband and a family. The sudden thought of having Michael's children brought her up with a jolt; stop being so stupid and illogical, she told herself fiercely, and put all such thoughts firmly to the back of your mind!

Resolutely following her own instructions, she set off for Heraklion airport to pick up Peter. Driving along the coast road, it was easy to forget about Michael—for one thing, the road was hazardous in many places and needed her concentration, and for another the scenery was spectacularly beautiful. The water was mirror-like in its calmness, so smooth the few ripples that did appear looked like clear blue silk. The air was fresh, with a hint of pleasant coolness so early in the morning, and Gabbie had the roof back so that the air rushed past her ears with a flyaway sensation.

In spite of Felicity's comments, for once the flight actually did arrive on time, spilling out its load of pale-skinned holidaymakers, who Gabbie knew would be returning to England in a week or two looking healthily tanned. She scanned the crowd anxiously for Peter, and saw him struggling to retrieve his luggage from the very erratic conveyor belt that lurched around in a semicircle, dropping off half the suitcases on its way. She grinned, remembering her own ordeal trying to catch up with her suitcases, as she watched Peter achieve his goal, then pass through the gates to look around for sight of her.

'I'm here!' Frantically she waved, trying to make

herself seen above the crush of people making their way out to buses and taxis.

'I thought I was going to spend the whole fort-night following my luggage around on that con-veyor belt,' said Peter when he finally reached her.

Gabbie giggled; he looked quite hot and bothered, unusual for him. 'Never mind, from now on just sit back and relax,' she told him as she kissed him fondly. 'It's lovely to see you.'

'You too,' said Peter, giving her a squeeze.

As it was Gabbie's day off, and Peter said he didn't feel in the least bit tired, they decided to stay in Heraklion for the day before returning to Aghios Nikolaos. Gabbie found a shady place to park the cark, beneath some fragrant eucalyptus trees near the bus station, then they made their way up the hill, past the Venetian fortress into the centre of the busy town of Heraklion.

First they had a drink, sitting in a little taverna, filled even at that early hour of the morning with old men in their black-fringed crocheted caps, clicking their worry beads and drinking the habitual coffee and ouzo.

'You know, I've never tried ouzo,' said Peter, looking curiously at the milky liquid in the tall glasses.

'There's always a first time,' said Gabbie, order-ing them both coffee and ouzo.

'Imagine drinking alcohol at this time of the morning in England,' said Peter, sipping it appre-ciately. 'You'd be classed as an alcoholic!' He looked around at the animated and yet relaxing scene in the bright morning sunlight.

'You like it?' asked Gabbie. 'The ouzo *and* Crete, I mean?'

'Yes, what I've seen of it so far,' said Peter, then he added slowly, 'But even so, I was wondering if . . .' he sighed and left the sentence unfinished.

'Wondering what?' Gabbie worried, what was wrong?

'Wondering whether perhaps I should have stayed in England, and not come here. You see, I've been thinking, even since Mother talked to me; I gather she wrote to you,' he added.

Gabbie nodded. 'Yes, but what has that got to do with staying in England?'

'Well . . . I've been wanting to get in touch with Sue, but to begin with my pride wouldn't let me, but every day it's been getting less and less—my pride, I mean; and now I'm filled with the urge to hold her in my arms, to tell her what a fool I've been.' He looked shamefacedly at Gabbie. 'In other words, to ask her forgiveness and promise that in future, I will *not* spend every waking hour at the hospital.'

Gabbie smiled delightedly. 'This holiday will do you good,' she said gently. 'I shall take care you don't lose that feeling, and soon you'll be able to tell Sue all those things. This holiday will set you up so that you're more relaxed, more than you've been for years.'

'Perhaps you're right,' said Peter, absent-mindedly toying with his coffee cup, his thoughts obviously still with Sue.

'I *am* right,' replied Gabbie positively, smiling secretly to herself. Little did Peter know how soon he would be able to hold Sue and tell her he loved her. Her plans were working out without, it seemed, much need for any help from her!

They spent a fascinating morning in the crowded street market, and Gabbie was glad to see that Peter seemed happier than she had seen him for a long time. Making up his mind to do something positive about his marriage had added a new dimension to his outlook on life, and together they sampled and explored the noisy maze of stalls and shops. When, feeling totally exhausted, they ate in a tiny side-street taverna, Gabbie would have preferred something slightly more luxurious, but Peter insisted they ate authentic Greek, as he said. As the taverna was full of workmen in their blue overalls, it was difficult to find anywhere more authentic, Gabbie agreed, and besides, the stuffed aubergines and crispy fried sardines *did* look delicious.

After lunch she drove him back to the cottage, where after just dumping his suitcases in the middle of his allotted bedroom, both Gabbie and Peter slumped on their beds in the heat of the afternoon, sleeping off the surfeit of aubergines and other delicacies they'd consumed.

Felicity still hadn't come back from work when they arose and freshened up. Peter complained a little about the lack of a bathroom, but not too much, Gabbie was glad to notice. Like her, he too was captivated by the view, agreeing that it more than made up for anything else that might be

missing. Gabbie agreed with him, but had difficulty
in concentrating on what Peter was saying; her
mind was on Felicity and Michael. Obviously they
must have decided to make another evening of it; it
was six o'clock, long past the time when she knew
Felicity was off duty. Determinedly she tried to put
all thoughts of both of them out of her mind. It was
inevitable, she had known it really, right from the
start. Felicity was very pretty and agreeable, and
what was more to the point, she didn't fight with
Michael, the way Gabbie had ever since that fatal
interview. Yes, she reflected resignedly, Felicity
would fit in very well with Michael's scheme
of things, into his idea of men and women's
place in life. He would be the master, and
Felicity would happily acquiesce, not continually
challenge as Gabbie had the inborn instinct to
do.

Once she had decided to accept the inevitable,
Gabbie found she relaxed, and spent a very
pleasant evening with Peter. They ate out at a
restaurant by the side of Lake Voulismeni, amusing
themselves by throwing bread at the teeming fish,
watching the water almost boil as the fish fought
over the pieces of bread. Then they returned to the
cottage very late. It was nearly midnight, and they
had stayed to watch a display of Greek dancing at
another restaurant along the sea-front away from
the tranquil lake.

The Calor gas lamp was burning low in the
kitchen, and Aphrodite greeted them with a loud
rumble of purring, and actually got out of her box

to greet them, her thin tail whiplashing affectionately around Gabbie's bare legs.

'You've got a friend for life there,' observed Peter.

'I know,' said Gabbie absently. She was reading a note propped up on the table, it was from Felicity.

> 'Sorry not to stay up to say hello to your brother, hope you two had a good day. I've had an absolutely BA one! MN was in a foul mood, he wasn't exactly all sweetness and light last night although I did my darnedest!!! The Institute is bursting at the seams with sick kids, there's an enteritis epidemic, so wear your plastic apron when you go in tomorrow! It might be a good idea to go in early, as our beloved Medical Director has been behaving like a starting marshal at the Grand Prix, timing everyone!
>
> Even Sam complained, so you can guess it must be bad!!'

Silently Gabbie passed the note to Peter, who read it and laughed. 'Sounds like you're in for a hard time tomorrow,' he said. 'You'd best get your beauty sleep right away. Don't worry about me tomorrow, I'll wander down somehow to Aghios Nikolaos and go and see Paulos, then we'll come back together when you've finished.'

Gabbie kissed her brother good night. 'Yes.' She was relieved that he didn't mind spending the day alone. 'Ask Felicity for a lift down, she won't mind,' she said as they went up the stairs, 'she's got all day off.'

Peter gave her the thumbs-up sign as they parted silently on the landing, not wanting to wake the exhausted Felicity, and Gabbie undressed and climbed into bed. She thought of Felicity's note, mentally re-reading it; half of her was pleased that Felicity and Michael obviously weren't romantically involved as she had thought, the other half was puzzled. Why was he in such a foul mood, was there some other reason? Or had he perhaps made advances to Felicity and she'd put him off? She smiled suddenly in the darkness. If indeed that was the case, then he'd be scoring up another notch against the English; that was of course if Sam was to be believed. Still puzzling, she fell asleep. It had been a long day and another one, not likely to be so enjoyable, loomed ahead.

Felicity's advice to wear a plastic apron turned out to be no exaggeration. There were two wards of children being sick, some very small babies indeed. Gabbie saw Michael, but the only words they exchanged were about the need, or otherwise, to put up drips on some of the badly dehydrated children. He, like her, and the other girls on duty, was completely immersed in the needs of the patients, but at least Gabbie noticed with relief that they only had two fresh admissions that day. It seemed that the epidemic had peaked and was now declining; and by the end of the day a tired but triumphant band of nurses, and Gabbie, felt they had the situation under control.

Before she left, Gabbie did a round of the two wards, caring for the children with gastro-enteritis. She had made up a strict rota of nurses, forbidding them to work on other wards, and forbade the girls not involved to even set foot in the infection wards. The last thing they needed was for the micro-organisms causing the outbreak to spread; cross-infection was always a danger, even more so where children were concerned. She had laid down a strict régime. Felicity had left a note in the office telling her she hadn't had time to do it the day before, so Gabbie wrote out the instructions herself.

She explained what barrier nursing techniques involved, telling the girls the essentials; the need to gown, frequent washing of hands, plastic bags to be sealed with all rubbish, and had pinned 'Enteric Precaution' cards on the doors of both wards. Putting in her own gown, and disposing of her plastic gloves in the bin for incineration, she hoped Michael wouldn't object to the extra expense incurred for the paper gowns. I suppose I'll have to ask his permission, she thought, walking slowly down the corridor, although she had already instructed the nurses to use them.

'You look worried. I thought we'd got over the hump with the outbreak?' Michael's voice interrupted her musing.

'I think we have,' said Gabbie, then deciding to take the bull by the horns, she added briskly, 'I hope you won't object to the extra cost of paper gowns. I've asked for some more to be delivered. I've instructed all the nurses involved in those two wards to use barrier nursing techniques. I feel it's essential to prevent cross-infection.'

To her immense relief Michael actually seemed pleased. 'Good,' he said, rewarding her with one of his flashing smiles. 'I had intended to ask you to do it, but as you know we've been a little pushed today.'

Gabbie smiled back, trying to ignore the pile-driver action of her heart; you are *not* going to go weak at the knees, she reminded herself with some asperity. 'I'll go now,' she said, 'if everything is quiet for the night.'

'Yes, everything is quiet,' replied Michael, but he didn't leave her side, just continued walking until they reached the entrance foyer of the Institute. Gabbie could see Peter waiting outside.

Raising her hand, she waved at him, and turned to say goodbye to Michael, only to find he had walked straight past her, out to where Peter was waiting. 'Did you have a good day swimming, Peter?' she heard him ask.

'Great,' said Peter. 'Felicity dropped me off at this little sandy beach, and I've spent the whole day either swimming or sleeping. I've just come from visiting Paulos, I must say he's making a wonderful recovery—it's amazing what willpower can do.'

'Oh yes,' agreed Michael, 'he has tremendous willpower, it runs in the family.'

You can say that again! thought Gabbie ruefully, wondering how it was that Michael knew Peter.

The explanation was not long in coming. 'Felicity introduced me to your brother—I had no idea he was *the* Peter from London that Paulos is always referring to. Why didn't you tell me it was your brother who was coming?'

'You didn't ask,' said Gabbie, feeling on the defensive. 'If I remember rightly, *you* jumped to conclusions, and promptly gave me a lecture on the villagers' moral attitudes!'

Peter roared with laughter. 'Do you mean to say you thought Gabbie was inviting a boyfriend to stay with her?' He laughed even more and hugged his sister. 'That'll be the day! She's a confirmed bachelor girl, always has been.'

'So she's told me, although I didn't believe her,' replied Michael, raising one dark brow in an ironic quirk. 'But if you ask me, Peter, it's a waste of a good woman. She could make some man happy, I'm sure.'

'Yes,' said Peter, releasing his sister and standing back to look at her. 'Yes,' he said again reflectively, 'she's not bad-looking really.'

'No, not bad at all,' said Michael in the same tone of voice.

'Oh, really, both of you!' Gabbie turned from one to the other. 'Stop talking about me as if I'm a pound of meat on a butcher's slab!'

'We measure in kilos here,' Michael reminded her, with a sudden wicked grin. He laughed. 'You know, that expression on your face reminds me of our first meeting. Really, Dr Nikolaides!' he mimicked her outraged tone of voice perfectly.

Gabbie turned away, blushing furiously; between the two of them they had her at a disadvantage. 'Let's go and eat,' she said quickly to Peter, and walked across to her car.

The next two days were unbearably hot. Maria assured Gabbie that it was a heatwave even for Crete. The Institute was still very busy, and the intense heat meant that their young enteritis patients were in constant danger of becoming dehydrated, so Michael kept most of them in bed with saline drips. Felicity and Gabbie had agreed between them that Gabbie would carry on with the organisation of the rest of the clinic, and Felicity would look after the two isolation wards with the enteritis patients.

It meant Gabbie didn't have the time off she was scheduled for, and as a result had to leave Peter to his own devices. He seemed happy enough when she saw him in the evenings, usually late by the time she got back; he'd spent his time swimming or talking to Paulos and Maria, who were very pleased to see a different face. On Tuesday evening when she got back to the cottage, it was deserted, no sign of either Felicity or Peter. There was a note from Peter, however, pinned to Aphrodite's box. It read: Having supper with Maria and Paulos, thought you wouldn't mind. Feeling a bit low today, missing Sue terribly. Peter.

Missing Sue terribly. Gabbie clapped her hand to her mouth. She'd completely forgotten Sue and Emma were arriving the next day, Wednesday, and she hadn't prepared Peter for their arrival! All her well-laid plans of gently talking to him, preparing the ground for a reconciliation, had gone by the board, swept aside in the sudden rush of extra work caused by the epidemic they'd been coping with. She waited and waited for Peter to come back that night, but there was no sign of either him or Felicity, so eventually she decided to change and lie on the bed while she waited, she felt so tired.

The next thing she knew was waking up to the clear blue light of dawn creeping in through her open window. She had fallen asleep, not even waking when they'd returned. Looking at her watch, she saw it was five o'clock. Sue and Emma were arriving at Heraklion at ten that morning. There was no question now of being able to break the news gently, there was nothing for it but to tell Peter and hope the news went down well!

Silently she crept downstairs, trying to be as quiet as possible. She'd make some coffee, take a cup up to Peter, then tell him. But even that plan was thwarted, for she had barely put the kettle on to boil when a bleary-eyed Peter staggered down into the kitchen.

'I thought I heard you,' he said, rubbing his eyes. 'Oh hell, I feel awful! I sat up half the night talking with Michael and Paulos, while they poured brandy down my throat. Felicity decided to sleep in at the Institute by the way, she was concerned about one of the babies, apparently, so Michael brought me back.'

'Oh,' said Gabbie, frantically scurrying around in the corners of her mind for the right words. How on earth could she tell him his wife would be arriving in a few hours?

'I think I'll go back to England,' said Peter gloomily. 'Both Michael and Paulos convinced me that I mustn't waste any more time, that I must talk to Sue, and the sooner the better. Perhaps I've left it too late already,' he added miserably.

'No, you haven't,' said Gabbie triumphantly. The fates had played right into her hands again. Picking up the car keys from the hook by the door, she tossed them at her startled brother. 'Here, take these. Drop me off at the Institute and then go and pick up Sue and Emma—they're arriving on the ten o'clock flight from Gatwick.'

The look of pure, unadulterated joy that suddenly exploded across her brother's face was reward enough for Gabbie. 'Why, you wretch!' he said, beaming from ear to ear. 'You've had this up your sleeve all the time and never said a word!'

'I did intend to, love,' said Gabbie gently. 'I was intending to tactfully pave the way, but somehow the work at the Institute took over and . . .'

'You don't have to do anything.' Peter picked her up and swung her around the kitchen in a violent circle, hugging and kissing her. 'I know what I've got to do. I've got to tell my wife and daughter that I love them both more than anything in the world, and that I've been a bloody fool!'

Gabbie laughed, pleased that her plans hadn't gone awry after all. 'Don't swear in front of Emma,' she teased.

'Michael told me last night,' said Peter, suddenly becoming serious, 'that when you find a woman you love, you've got to hang on to her, no matter what the obstacles might be. You've got to convince her that you love her more than life itself.'

'Very good advice,' said Gabbie dryly, 'but he's hardly an authority on the subject, is he!'

'Oh, I don't know,' shrugged Peter. 'From what he said last night I think he's got his eyes on someone, and is working around to it in his own way.'

'Oh,' said Gabbie.

'Probably Felicity,' said Peter, echoing Gabbie's own thoughts. He sipped the coffee she passed to him. 'She's a very attractive girl, and a thoroughly nice one too. I expect he doesn't want to rush her.'

'Yes, she is nice,' agreed Gabbie. Suddenly she shivered as a cloud crossed the sun, the forerunner of a storm, if the black clouds on the horizon were anything to go by.

CHAPTER ELEVEN

PETER dropped Gabbie off at the Institute as planned, then went on his way, looking extremely happy at the prospect of meeting Sue and Emma; Gabbie tried to cheer herself up by feeling pleased for him, but a black cloud of despondency seemed to have settled over her. She felt tired and dispirited, her whole body seemed leaden.

'Isn't the heat awful?' said Felicity, wandering into the office holding an iced coffee for each of them. 'I've brought you one of these, as I thought perhaps you might be feeling as rotten as I do.'

Gabbie took the tall glass and swished the ice cubes round in the creamy liquid gratefully. Of course, how silly of her—that was it, the heat combined with the extreme humidity was enough to get anyone down. It cheered her up considerably to find Felicity admitting to feeling tired and strangely depressed as well.

After chatting for a few minutes, Felicity informing her of the children's progress on the isolation wards. 'Most are doing quite well,' she said, 'but there are two small babies I'm worried about. The infection has passed, but it's left them so weak.' She looked worried. 'I've left them both on saline drips, but they're losing so much through perspiration that it's a battle to keep their fluid balance anything like normal.'

'Perhaps we'll have a storm, if those clouds are any indication,' said Gabbie, 'and then the air will clear.' They both looked out of the window. The normally sunny vista was dark and gloomy, heavy black clouds hung threateningly overhead, but as yet not a drop of rain had fallen.

'Ah well,' Felicity got up to go, 'let's keep our fingers crossed and hope it will rain eventually.'

Gabbie left her office to do the usual ward round, but first she hurried across to Maria and Paulos, to tell them the good news about Sue and Emma arriving.

Maria threw up her hands in delight. 'I had a feeling,' she announced. 'I knew everything would be all right!'

'You always have feelings like that,' grumbled Paulos, but he was smiling. He looked at Gabbie, who was on her way back to the Institute, dashing out of the door. 'You're a dark horse,' he said with a slow grin. 'Michael was right.'

'Michael?' said Gabbie, stopping in the doorway and looking back. 'What do you mean?'

'Oh, Michael says,' blurted out Maria before Paulos could stop her, 'that you are not a bit like you appear. He said, "Still waters run deep" and that the saying applies to you.'

'Quite the philosopher,' said Gabbie, pulling a face, and wondering what else Michael might have said to his parents. 'However, I hate to disappoint you, but I am *exactly* as I appear, there's nothing complicated about me!'

She sped back to the Institute, uncomfortably aware of the knowing smile Maria and Paulos had exchanged, almost as if they knew something she didn't. But once there, the morning was so hectic that she completely forgot about their strange behaviour. Apart from the isolation wards, the whole Institute was full, having had more than its normal quota of trauma admissions.

'Why is it all the children fall off their bikes and break arms and legs all at the same time?' grumbled Sam, having just come out of theatre on to the ward. 'I've just pinned and plated I don't know how many fractures.'

'School holidays now,' Eleni reminded him, 'the children have more time to play.' She looked at her watch. 'Oh, before I go to see Mrs Haidis, Dr Nikolaides asked me to ask if you could do the general outpatient session, it's due to start in ten minutes. He is still tied up in the isolation ward.'

Sam groaned. 'What have I done to deserve this?' he moaned, putting his head in his hands. 'And why can't we have a storm to get rid of some of this wretched heat?'

Gabbie echoed his sentiments on that score, neither of them guessing their wishes were about to be granted. 'Do you want me to give you a hand with the clinic?' she asked, looking at the chart with the nursing rota on the ward wall. Heleanna was down to assist, and although she was extremely keen, she was still relatively inexperienced; it took her longer to prepare the patients than some of the other girls.

'You're on, honey,' said Sam, taking her up on her word.

There were forty-five patients scheduled to be seen, and Sam muttered and grumbled about Michael always overbooking. 'I'd have only seen half this number,' he said.

'Well, there's not much option now,' said Gabbie. 'They're all here, by the look of it.'

'Yes, plus mothers, fathers *and* grandmothers,' replied Sam, looking at the crowd morosely.

Gabbie smiled. It was true. The clinic was one of the free ones run by Michael, and most of the patients came from the surrounding rural villages, and as was their custom the entire family turned up.

The clinic started, and Sam had only got to the second patient when it began to rain. Although Gabbie thought the word rain didn't describe it very well, monsoon would have been more like it! The rain came down in straight sheets, so thick and heavy it was almost impossible to see across from the Institute to the villa. The oleanders and hibiscus bowed to the ground under the weight of water, and the thunder and lightning seemed to almost rock the building.

'I said I wished it would rain,' said Sam, looking out of the window to where a great pool had suddenly appeared where once had been lawn, 'I didn't ask for a hurricane!'

Gabbie had other thoughts on her mind, however. 'What about the patients and their relatives?'

she asked. 'They can't possibly leave the Institute while it's like this.'

'You'd better make arrangements with Olga in the *kafénion*,' said Sam in a resigned tone of voice. 'Tell her to provide cold drinks and biscuits for the children and coffee for the adults. But they'll have to stay in the waiting area, we can't have them flooding out the *kafénion*.'

'Choose your words more carefully,' said Gabbie, looking at the downpour. 'At this rate everything will be flooded!'

After organising refreshments for the captive outpatients and relatives, she and Sam finished the session. It was hard work getting through forty-five patients, but somehow between them they managed it, and finished late in the afternoon.

Together they made their way through the outpatient waiting area. The din was ear-splitting, adults carrying on conversations at the top of their voices, and children crying.

'I'm glad I didn't let them into the *kafénion*,' said Sam.

Gabbie was glad too, at least the *kafénion* provided some sort of refuge from the rest of the Institute, which she felt would burst at the seams any moment if they weren't able to get rid of some of its inhabitants. She and Sam sat down together to a very late lunch. Sam manfully wading through a mountain of moussaka, his favourite, while Gabbie toyed with a Greek salad. How Sam could eat when it was so hot she didn't know.

They were at the far end of the room, furthest

away from the counter, and they both saw Michael and Felicity come in. Felicity was talking animatedly, and Michael was laughing. Gabbie's heart slumped like a lead balloon into her toes when she saw Michael playfully slip an arm around Felicity's petite waist.

Sam had noticed too. 'I thought I had it made there,' he said gloomily. 'Felicity led me on to think I was quite attractive.'

'You'll just have to work harder to convince her,' said Gabbie lightly, desperately submerging the jealous pang that seared through her. 'Try being absolutely devastatingly attractive. You'll just have to give her one of those flashing smiles Michael is so good at!'

'Oh, so you've noticed,' said Sam curiously. 'I thought you were quite immune.'

'Oh, I am, I am,' replied Gabbie hastily, anxious that he shouldn't get the wrong impression, 'but that doesn't stop me noticing how he uses it to effect on other women!'

An hour later the storm abated, and the Institute discharged its reluctant guests. They spilled out on to the gravel path outside the building, skirting the massive puddles, chattering like a flock of starlings as they made their way, en masse, out through the Institute gates.

Along with most of the other staff Gabbie heaved a huge sigh of relief; life could begin to return to something like normal. She looked at her watch and saw with surprise that it was time for her to go off duty. She hadn't seen Felicity for some time, and presumed she had probably left the minute it had stopped raining and gone back to the cottage, as she should have had the afternoon off.

Before she left, she dashed to the other end of the building for her daily visit to Mrs. Haidis. Her husband had returned to their village now, and Mrs Haidis would be going soon; the babies were strong and crying lustily for their feeds when she arrived. Smiling, Gabbie asked Mrs Haidis how she was, in halting Greek, and was pleased she managed to understand her reply. Then, looking at the notes, she saw that Michael had written a note about the possibility of discharge the following day.

One mission very successfully completed, she thought as she sought out Sam, who was to drive her back to the cottage as Peter still had her car. On the way back she wondered how the three of them were getting on, and where they had spent the time during the awful storm—somewhere safe and dry in Heraklion, she hoped. Sam drove her up to the cottage, dropping her on the roadside, before reversing and returning to the Institute.

On arrival inside the cottage she found it awash. The water had run down the mountainside, through the little front door, which they never used, flooded the kitchen before seeping out under the kitchen door, to join up with the rest of the storm water running down to the sea.

Gabbie's first thought was for Aphrodite. There was so much water in the kitchen that she thought perhaps she and her kitten had been drowned, the water escaping with the whoosh of a mini-tidal wave when she opened the kitchen door. But she need not have worried. Aphrodite, good little mother that she was, had carried her baby upstairs and was sitting snugly in the middle of Gabbie's bed; which was just as well, as the cardboard box she had previously occupied had disintegrated, and floated down the hill with the rest of the water when Gabbie had opened the door; she had managed to rescue the yellow cardigan and pegged that out on the line to dry. The sun was shining now, and everything was steaming like a tropical rain forest.

There was no sign of Felicity, and Gabbie stood disconsolately looking at the mess, wondering where to start mopping up first; then she heard the familiar sound of her own car and knew Peter and his family were about to arrive.

There were kisses all round, and some tears from Sue. Peter looked flushed and happy, and Emma, squealing with excitement at the sight of all the mud and water, which she adored, plus the fact that her parents were together again, ran around diving into everything, laughing excitedly.

'I've arranged for a taxi to come up in about ten minutes,' said Peter. 'If you don't mind we'll leave Emma with you, and Sue and I will stay in a hotel down in Aghios Nikolaos—we've still got a lot of talking to do.'

Emma hung on to Gabbie's hand excitedly, pleased to stay, and Peter and Sue were so busy looking at each other that Gabbie knew they hadn't even noticed the fact that the kitchen was awash with mud!

The taxi duly arrived and Peter and Sue piled in, waved off by a happy Emma and a not quite so happy Gabbie, who was still thinking about the mess she had to clear up somehow. After they had gone, she and Emma set to work with stiff brooms, and managed to sweep out most of the mud, although everything was still wet. Felicity hadn't come back, so after feeding Aphrodite, Gabbie decided to take Emma down to Aghios Nikolaos to eat—anything to get away from the wet mess for a while. She hoped things would have dried out a little by the time they got back.

Before finding a restaurant she took Emma in to see Maria and Paulos, knowing how they loved children. 'I have your rooms all ready,' said Maria as soon as she saw them. 'You can't stay at your house until tomorrow. It will be dry by then.'

'But how . . . ?'

'Felicity went up briefly after the storm to make sure your cat was all right, and she came back and told me. She's sleeping in the Institute, and Peter and Sue have already been in, although they didn't mention the flooding.'

Gabbie smiled. 'They're so happy, I don't think they even noticed,' she said.

Maria was so insistent, and Gabbie felt tired; besides, she could see the logic of Emma having somewhere decent to sleep for the night, so without much of a struggle she gave in, secretly relieved that she didn't have to face the waterlogged kitchen for another few hours at least.

After supper on the patio, Gabbie put Emma to

bed. She wondered where Michael had been. He
hadn't joined them for supper. Working, she supposed, or with Felicity. Emma fell asleep almost
before Gabbie had left the room. It had been a
momentous day for her—up at the crack of dawn,
flying to Crete, her parents reconciling and then
being flooded out! Quite an eventful day for one
little girl, thought Gabbie with a smile.

The air was warm, but felt clear and clean now,
so Gabbie joined Paulos and Maria on the patio for
a drink. It was pleasant sitting in the subdued
lamplight just talking; then Paulos decided it was
time for bed. With Maria hovering anxiously behind, he determinedly made his way into the villa,
leaning on his walking frame, but managing unaided.

Gabbie sat on alone, listening to the sounds of
the night, the plip-plop of water still dripping from
some of the thick-leaved bushes, the heady fragrance of jasmine flooding the still air. Michael
appeared at last, and came and sat beside her, and
poured himself an ouzo.

'I understand you're staying the night,' he said.

'Yes, we've been flooded out,' replied Gabbie.

'It will be dry by tomorrow,' he said. 'Those little
mountain cottages are built with the doors like that
so that the water can run straight through.'

'Oh,' said Gabbie, feeling suddenly tonguetied.

'I feel like a stroll,' said Michael, 'after being
cooped up all day in that heat. I need some exercise
—want to come?'

To her surprise Gabbie heard herself agreeing,

and together they walked slowly through the gardens. The lawn was almost dry again now, the pool of water soaking into the parched earth, the perfume of the jasmine mixed with the sharp aromatic fragrance of the bruised leaves of the citrus trees gave out a magical scent. They strolled around in a big circle, and took a path between the villa and the Institute, where the hibiscus bushes grew thickly, their fragrant bell-shaped flowers hanging overhead.

Suddenly Michael put his hands on Gabbie's shoulders and swung her round to face him. She could just make out the planes and angles of his face in the dim starlight.

'You purposely let me think your brother was a boyfriend,' he said accusingly.

The sudden confrontation with the truth threw Gabbie, and she searched desperately for some sort of plausible answer, but ended in only saying rather lamely, 'Well, what if I did? It doesn't make any difference to you, does it?'

'You know damn well it does!' said Michael roughly. 'This should tell you why.'

He bent his head and kissed her very gently, taking Gabbie completely by surprise. His mouth tasted faintly of the ouzo he had been drinking, or was it her ouzo? She couldn't remember, couldn't think straight, not with his warm lips on hers, his arms holding her so close she could feel the beating of his heart through the thin cotton of his shirt.

'You see,' he said softly, 'that's the reason why it makes a difference.'

'But I . . .' mumbled Gabbie, trying to equate this gentle tender Michael with the one who frequently quarrelled with her, or the one who had kissed her so passionately she'd felt as if she would explode! 'But what about Felicity . . .' she began.

'What about Felicity?' he replied, pulling her closer. 'She's probably talking to Sam—she's crazy about him, you know.'

'No, I didn't. I . . .'

'I've come to the conclusion you don't know much,' said Michael severely, 'including what you really think yourself. It's about time matters were rectified.' With that, his arms tightened around her, and his mouth found hers with a slow deliberation.

Slowly, trembling a little, Gabbie relaxed and slid her arms around his neck, her eyes closed as shock wave after shock wave of pleasure swept through her body as his kiss deepened and intensified. The touch of his mouth against hers, the pressure of his body, sent a deep piercing sensual excitement shuddering through her, as with total abandonment now, she parted her lips for his invading tongue.

The ground beneath their feet seemed to shake. I never really thought the earth would move, thought Gabbie hazily, kissing him back with a hunger that matched his.

It was only when he suddenly broke away from her, and the earth continued to shake, that she realised it was not the kiss that had caused it. 'It's an earthquake,' said Michael tersely. 'Come on, we've got to get back to the Institute.'

Together they ran, brushing aside the dripping wet trees, trying to ignore the unreal feeling of the earth swaying beneath their feet. It only lasted a few seconds, but to Gabbie, who had never experienced an earthquake before, it seemed like a lifetime. As they neared the Institute, the violent rocking of the earth stopped, but at the same time the ominous rumble and crash of falling masonry could be heard. It came from the far end of the building.

'It's Mrs Haidis's room,' said Michael, running.

Gabbie's first instinct was to scream when she saw the pile of rubble at the end of the building where Mrs Haidis had been in the upstairs room. But all her professional training rose to the fore, and with Michael at her side, she began to help him remove the rubble. They were all still alive, that much they knew because they could hear both babies crying, and Mrs Haidis was calling out for help, in a desperate frightened voice.

Michael shouted something in Greek and Mrs Haidis was quiet, although the babies continued to cry. 'What did you say?' asked Gabbie quietly.

'I told her to be quiet and save her energy, because we don't want any more masonry falling,' said Michael.

Other helpers joined them, including Sam, but Michael told him to go back to the Institute to check on the wellbeing of the other patients. He disappeared, and Michael gave a satisfied sigh. 'The building has withstood the shock well,' he said. 'The steel reinforcing has formed a little cave, so they all seem to be OK.'

He had had a torch in his pocket and was flashing it into the dark cavern. Slowly Gabbie squeezed in behind Michael, and he passed her the first baby. In turn she passed it to Sophie, who was waiting outside, her arms stuck through the hole they had made. Then with the same painstaking care they slowly retrieved the other baby, bawling lustily, Gabbie, noted with relief.

'Now for Mrs Haidis,' muttered Michael. 'This will be a little more difficult.'

'Let me go in front of you,' said Gabbie. 'I'm smaller, I . . .'

'No, it's too dangerous!' The words were snapped out sharply and Gabbie knew there was no point in arguing, and anyway there wasn't time. So with her heart in her mouth she watched by the dim light of the torch as Michael pulled away more rubble and manoeuvred himself behind Mrs Haidis. Then slowly, slowly he began to edge her towards Gabbie, who took her head and shoulders and eased her body out through the opening.

With a sigh of relief she and Sophie gently lifted the young mother's body on to a waiting stretcher, then Gabbie looked back, expecting to see Michael's head appear. But instead of Michael's head and shoulders, there was a sudden crack and a great plume of dust spewed forth from the hole, as the remainder of the ceiling caved in.

'Michael!' screamed Gabbie, flinging herself at the hole through which she had last seen him.

CHAPTER TWELVE

THE NEXT twenty minutes seemed like something from a terrible, unreal nightmare. Impervious to her own safety and to the cries of Sophie and the others around to be careful, Gabbie determinedly crawled back into the ruins.

'Pass me a torch,' she whispered back to Sophie, afraid the echoes from her voice might bring more masonry crashing down. Obediently Sophie passed a torch through the opening.

'I'm going to get Sam,' she said, but Gabbie didn't wait to hear.

She was too busy trying to find Michael amidst the pile of plaster, bricks and steel girders. It was so quiet, it frightened her. He must be dead, she thought, cold beads of fear breaking out on her forehead, as she frantically swung the torch around looking for some sign of him. Then she heard a faint sound, and saw a little puff of dust away to the right. Quickly she slithered through the narrow gap, and then to her horror saw Michael's hair protruding up through a layer of fine, sandy plaster. His head was buried—he must be suffocating!

'Don't die, don't die,' she muttered feverishly under her breath, trying not to cry as she clawed away at the fine powdery dust. Careless of the bricks and steel scraping at her own face and body, causing blood to pour down her arms and legs, she managed to free Michael's head, and slid a finger down to feel the pulse in his neck.

There was nothing, nothing! Panic as she had never known it before flooded through her, but desperately she tried to subdue it so that she could think clearly, think positively. Then, twisting her body into an excruciating position, she managed to reach his face, and started mouth-to-mouth resuscitation. Doggedly she persisted, vaguely aware of the girders being manhandled away by many willing hands, and then of Sam beside her.

'I'll take over now,' he said grimly, pushing an oxygen mask on to Michael's face.

By now there were other men there too, they had lanterns and there was plenty of light. Gently and slowly they extricated Michael from the ruins of the room that had once been the little maternity ward. Only Gabbie didn't see it, she had collapsed in a dead faint, from her injuries and sheer fatigue.

She came round momentarily, to find herself on a stretcher, being carried away from the scene. Desperately she pulled herself up, trying to get off, to get back, to find out what had happened to Michael—was he alive or dead? But strong hands restrained her.

'I'll examine her,' she heard Paulos's voice saying from a great distance, 'find out what's broken.' Nothing is broken on me, she wanted to cry out, but the words wouldn't come, and she lapsed back into unconsciousness again.

When she finally awoke it was to find Sophie sitting at her bedside. 'What . . . ?' she began.

'Shush!' said Sophie soothingly, pushing her gently back against the pillows. 'Dr Paulos says you are not to move.'

'But Michael . . . ?' The full horror of the earthquake and its aftermath came flooding back.

'Michael is all right. Dr Paulos will come and see you now—I'll tell him you are awake. Promise me not to move.'

'I promise,' said Gabbie slowly, looking around the room. It was still dark outside, so it couldn't be long after the earthquake, she reasoned. Then she tried to move slightly in the bed and found everything hurt, and to her surprise she also found she was bandaged quite extensively. That's funny, she thought, still feeling slightly bemused, I don't remember getting hurt.

The door to her room opened and Paulos came in, leaning heavily on his walking frame. 'Oh, Paulos,' protested Gabbie, 'you shouldn't be up at this time of night, and after the earthquake too!'

'I've been up for several nights,' said Paulos with a lopsided smile, 'looking after you and my son, and it doesn't seem to have done me any harm.'

'How is Michael?' asked Gabbie urgently.

Slowly Paulos lowered himself gently on to the side of the bed, taking care not to sit on her. 'He's alive, and apart from two cracked ribs very well. Thanks to you.' He reached out and took her hand. 'I know what happened that awful night—you saved his life. Sam told me that if you hadn't gone on giving mouth-to-mouth resuscitation he would never have survived.'

'That awful night?' repeated Gabbie slowly. 'Then it wasn't tonight?'

Paulos laughed gently. 'My dear, you were more badly hurt than you realised. You suffered concussion yourself, and many cuts and grazes. We've been quite worried about you.'

'I don't remember getting hurt,' said Gabbie, frowning.

'No, because you ignored it—you had one blind instinct driving you on, to save life. Someone else's life, not your own,' said Paulos.

'When can I . . . ?'

'See Michael?' Paulos finished for her with a chuckle. 'Tomorrow, my dear. He's only in the next room, you can see him tomorrow.' He got up laboriously from the bed. 'Now drink this drink Sophie has for you and get a good night's sleep. I'll see you in the morning.'

Obediently Gabbie took the drink from Sophie, and under her watchful eye drank it all after Paulos had left. Then she slid down back on the soft pillows with a sigh.

'Good night,' said Sophie softly, switching the main light off, just leaving on the dim night light.

'Good night,' said Gabbie.

After Sophie had gone she lay there, thinking about Michael. Had he really only cracked two ribs, were they telling her the truth? Suddenly she sat up in bed. She had to see him for herself, to see that he really was alive and well.

Slipping on the dressing gown that was draped over the chair at the side of the bed, Gabbie slowly and rather painfully slid out of bed. She felt a little shaky for the first few steps, but then gained confidence. She would just creep into Michael's room, his father had said he was next door, just take a look for herself to make sure that he was as they had told her; he would be sleeping like everyone else, so she wouldn't disturb him, only look.

Slowly she crept into his room in her bare feet, after easing the door open and closing it quietly behind her. Then she walked across to the bed and stood looking down at him. He was asleep as she had expected, and she stood looking with loving eyes at his dark features, which somehow managed to look compelling even though he had his eyes closed.

Softly she reached out a hand and brushed it against his cheek. 'I love you, Michael,' she whispered, the words coming as if they were the most natural words in the world. She could acknowledge it to herself at last. She loved him.

His hand came up, imprisoning hers. 'You don't know how long I've waited to hear you say that,' he said, his black eyes wide awake and looking at her. 'Even since I first kissed you, in fact.'

'You weren't asleep at all!' said Gabbie accusingly.

'No,' he grinned, looking like his old self, 'but if I'd been obviously awake, you'd have muttered some excuse and beaten a hasty retreat, wouldn't you?'

'Probably,' admitted Gabbie, 'but only because I wouldn't have known what to say.'

'You've just said what I wanted to hear,' he said, 'and I love you too, Miss Kempson.' He raised her hand to his lips and kissed each finger slowly; each kiss, and Gabbie's heart did a double somersault.

'Now,' he said, throwing back the covers, 'get in.'

'Get in? What, here?' squeaked Gabbie. 'Oh, I couldn't! It isn't . . .'

'Get in!' His voice rang with the familiar note of command, the one she had rebelled against so often before. 'And mind my cracked ribs!'

Obediently Gabbie slid into bed beside him, slipping her good right arm underneath him. Slowly he pulled her towards him, sliding his right hand inside the dressing gown, inside the thin cotton of the nightdress until his hand was resting on the warm contour of her breast. 'I love you,' he said again.

The touch of his hand on her breast was doing the most incredible thing to the tempo of her heart and her breathing. 'Suppose someone comes in?' she gasped.

'They won't,' he said, as with infinite tenderness he began to kiss her, and Gabbie felt ripple after ripple of love and longing flood through her.

'I really don't think . . .' she breathed.

'Stop thinking for once, and just do what your senses tell you—we'll sort out the other details later.'

'What other details?' whispered Gabbie between

kisses, running the fingers of her left hand through the curly black hair on his chest.

'Oh, the date of the wedding, how many children we'll have, the formal adoption of Aphrodite and her brat, small things like that.'

'The date of the wedding? But . . .'

'I'm old-fashioned,' Michael told her severely. 'You don't think I would have invited you into my bed if I didn't intend to marry you.'

'Oh, really . . .'

'. . . Dr Nikolaides,' said Michael, mimicking her voice. 'Do stop talking, Sister, and concentrate on kissing!'

With a sigh Gabbie snuggled closer, turning her mouth to his. Yes, there was no doubt about it, kissing was much better than talking.